GW00859298

Death in a No

4

Only The Dead Die Twice
By Peter Mckeirnon

ISBN-10: 1986646556
ISBN-13: 978-1986646550

Cover designed by Wise Owl Imagery – Ian Hewitt.

Proof read by Kathryn Begley.

Undeadications Page

Donna Sayce, Selina Thomas, Dan Sutcliffe, Gemma Flynn, Christine Lunt, Paul Lancaster, Lisa Watson, Jenson Cross, Richard Wagner, Maisey Wagner, Denise Wagner, Ste Baker, James Baker, Suzie Baker, Lynda Baker, Alan Baker, Lucy Mannering, Stuart Davies, Elaine McCabe, Krys Kamenou, Abby Webb, Michelle Hankinson, Skippy Ransom and his brother Finlay, Caroline Ouseley, Tyler Ouseley, Kieran Ouseley, Susan Mathieson, James Quadir, Robert Quadir, Andrew Lennon, Hazel Lennon, Giles Batchelor, Mark Nye, Namey McNameface, Sharon Connolly, Tony Greenhalgh, Daniel Greenhalgh, Kelly Rickard, In memory of Lynne Beck, Sean Gunnery-Hitchen, Michelle Brown, Roy Brown, Rita Brown, Layla Carson, Mandi Varrie, Chris Mould, Lexi Mould, Sandra Sanpie Looker, Andy Coffey, Klaus Der Kranken, Jason White, Amy White, Benjamin Clarke, Katie Osborn, Sam Jones, Dave Jones, Finn Jones, Tim Oakes, Wendy Osborne, Tanya Evans, Chloe Houghton, Gareth Lees, Lisa Unsworth, Kathy Pepper, Nicky Jean Robinson, Judith Neale, Kev Slater, Liz Birch, Louise Birch, Joanne Berry, Harvey Berry, Kirky James Monsterwicz, Darren Anstey, Mick Tolley, Anthony Ehlen, Lucas Dockerty, Tracy Dockerty, Amber Lane, Tony, Alfie and Charlie Harris.

For Alex and Rowan.

Journal Entry 1

My name is John Daint. Father to a troubled teenage daughter, brother to a Spam obsessed, apocalypse loving lunatic and friend to a retro Scouser that likes to dream about a 20ft statue of Tina Turner that can fart cigarettes out of her arse. Not too long ago something terrible happened. People began to get sick. So sick that their internal organs systematically began to fail and they died in the most ghastly (and smelly) ways imaginable. Only they didn't stay dead and it wasn't long before the town I once knew became the nightmare my brother had warned me about. Zombies, deaders, walkers, shufflers or as 80s Dave so eloquently calls them, dead fucks, now roam our streets and the human race has become an endangered species. At least in Runcorn we have anyway. Who knows what's going on in the rest of the country? Maybe the military have been fighting back and are gaining control. Moving from city to city wiping out the hordes. Maybe once the cities are secure they'll move on to the smaller towns and we'll be saved. It's something I have found myself thinking about more and more of late. It's giving me something to hold on to, so I can see a light at the end of this blood and brain splattered tunnel.

I made the mistake of telling Butty about my hopes for a zombie free future and this was his response...

"Don't talk shite little brother. If the military had any kind of control over this we would have heard something by now. Gun fire, bombs, RAF fighter jets in the sky… there has been nothing. Not one indication that we are fighting back. No, we're in this for the long haul John. The only way through this is to survive the best we can and let things run their natural course. Give it five years or so and those of us that are still left will have gained the upper hand. By that time there will be no fresh zombies and the bastards that are still roaming will be so rotten they'll be easy pickings and barely a threat. Shame really."

Five years! Please let him be wrong for once. I seriously fear for my sanity if I have to spend half a decade roughing it with Butty and 80s Dave. I'm already beginning to assess situations like the terrible twosome. It was only a few hours ago that I found myself drawing up plans for my own homemade zombie armour whilst humming the theme tune to Airwolf.

I'm convinced the only thing stopping my head from going west is Emily. She is still very much suffering from the loss of Jonathon and everything we have gone through with Ged and his gang. It's going to take some time before she is anything like the girl she used to be and it breaks my heart to see her so withdrawn. I'm hoping that now we have Sophie and Gaby with us they will be a much needed positive influence and Emily can help to take care of them. Nick looks like he needs all the help he can get with the girls and I would rather my daughter spent her time helping with kids than killing zombies with her dad and crazy uncle.

To say we've not had much luck with the survivors we have met so far would be an understatement. Either they have been complete psychopaths or they have ended up dead and in some cases both. It's difficult not to develop a complex when everyone around you bites the big one. The only one that doesn't appear to share the burden is Butty but that shouldn't come as a surprise to anyone that has read my journals. Although, since we arrived at 'Apocalypse Street' and he's hooked up with Skywatcher, I have noticed a change in his behaviour. Could my survivalist, people hating, end of the world loving brother be becoming a little bit 'human'? Zombies roam the streets so I guess anything is possible!

It's been an eventful journey to get to where we are. We've lost loved ones, survived a house fire, tackled motorcycle maniacs, a crazy shit with a decapitated head for a best friend, met a mysterious girl with a cape and a hulk fist who literally saved our lives before buggering off before we could say thank you. We've witnessed zombie ducks, Barry refusing to close his shop during a zombie outbreak, my brother wear a lampshade around his neck. 80s Dave's Walkman melted and so did half of his battle paddle but like a gift from the Gods (well, Butty), we unearthed a replacement tape player and his new spear headed paddle has proved to be a formidable weapon. I lost my daughter twice, ate more Spam in a week than I have in my entire life, wore my boss's head as slippers and unintentionally became intimate with a zombie. At least I'm not as squeamish as I used to be!

But after everything we've been through, Emily, Butty, Dave and I, we're still together and our little group has grown in numbers with the addition of Nick, young Sophie and baby Gaby. And then there is Skywatcher, my brother's crush and the reason I'm sat here in relative comfort writing this journal. If it wasn't for her taking us in, God only knows where we would have ended up. Probably still hiding out in the old woman's apartment with hundreds of dead fucks outside. Instead here we are, once again in a house completely covered in zombie limbs and for the first time since the shit hit the fan, I'm feeling more human than I thought possible.

I woke this morning with my eyes still closed and my head sunken into the centre of a large fluffy pillow and what's more I was warm. Warm! Man I'd almost forgotten what it felt like to be anything but cold. The chord on the sleeping bag Skywatcher had given me was pulled tight and the heat inside had relaxed my muscles so much that my body shut down and I had fallen into a heavy and much needed sleep. The only reason I was awake was because I could hear Dave humming loudly along to music pumping out of his headphones.

"Let me guess. Gary Numan again?" I slurred, squeezing a hand out of my sleeping bag to wipe a slither of dribble from my chin and loosen the chord.

"Not today Ace. Whilst you were snoring your head off dreaming of mayo I got to thinking. Every day could be my last. We've seen a lot of death lately kid and let's be honest, it's been fucking grim. The world being the way it is, I could go at any time so I've decided that each day my listening pleasure shall be dedicated to my favourite musical artists of all time. First up Duran Duran. Fucking awesome lar. Five plucky lads from Birmingham that took the New Romantic scene by storm in the early 80s. Great pop anthems, great hair and awesome videos. You can't whack Duran Duran kidda. So today I am listening to nothing but le Bon and co. I was thinking of starting with Spandau Ballet but I wouldn't wish a full day of Tony Hadley on my worst enemy. Right, I'm off outside for a quick smoke. Did you know this Skywatcher bird has banned me from sparking up inside? There are zombies everywhere and she's making me go outside for a tab. Not to mention it's colder than a witches' tit! I need my own gaff John, somewhere I can be left to be awesome in peace and smoke as many biftas as I want. Which reminds me, Butty wants everyone in the control room in five minutes to discuss plans to fortify Electric Avenue."

"Control room?" I asked, stretching my upper body out of the sleeping bag.

"The Kitchen. Your brother's words not mine. I think he's finally gone loco kid. See you in five..." Dave said, grabbing his battle paddle and placing an unlit cigarette in his mouth before leaving the room.

Sluggishly I lifted my legs out of the sleeping bag and with heavy steps I walked to the bedroom window and looked to the street outside. It was quiet with not a shuffler to be seen. Skywatcher, under my brother's tutelage, had gone to town with securing her home. So much so that she made Butty look like an amateur. Zombie limbs covered so much of her house it was difficult to see the brick underneath and for extra protection, wooden stakes had been hammered into the ground, lining the perimeter of the building. She had worked tirelessly to make her home as safe as possible. A true Butty approved apocalyptic fortress.

Beyond the small cul-de-sac I could see fields and a nearby water tower. Our journey had taken us from the centre of Runcorn to its edges and an area of my town I was not familiar with and knew almost nothing about. The view from the window was alien to me. I could have been anywhere.

Hovering just above the fields that surrounded the water tower was a thick mist and within the mist zombies shuffled aimlessly, spread out sporadically in every direction. It was an eerie and frightening thing to see but it was also hypnotic. No matter how much it chilled me I couldn't take my eyes from the zombies, their lower bodies hidden, engulfed by the mist.

Then out of the corner of my eye I saw something thick and long swing down in front of the window, swaying freely from side to side. It was a zombie penis, blue and rigid with torn skin. It had been nailed to the wall above the window and had come loose. Whoever the owner of the cock was must have been a happy chap as it was bloody massive! Honestly, it looked like something out of Tremors! I bet it would be easy enough to find out who it belonged to. All I'd have to do is step outside and look at the decapitated heads nailed to the walls. Whichever looked the smuggest would be the former owner of the massive flopper.

Then a voice came from downstairs.

"Hey, little brother. Get your lazy arse downstairs. Everyone's waiting for you in the control room."

I pulled myself away from the pendulum-like knob swinging in front of the window and walked down stairs. I could hear Butty talking in the kitchen accompanied by the sound of flirtatious giggles from Skywatcher. He was slagging me off, making himself look big and tough at my expense. I could only make out the odd word but with those words being 'Throw-up merchant', 'Chocolate teapot', only alive because of me' and 'must have been adopted' it wasn't hard for me to figure out who he was bleating on about. Especially when I opened the door to the kitchen to find Skywatcher, Nick, Sophie, with little Gaby, lapping up my brother's tales. When they noticed me in the doorway the kitchen quickly fell silent.

"Morning big brother, have you made any coffee or are you drinking your own piss again?"

I thought that would wipe the smug look off his face and show Skywatcher how much of a basket case he really is but right on cue, she produced a large bottle of urine and gulped it down like it was nectar from the gods. I could have puked but I didn't want to give Butty the satisfaction.

"I hope that's your own and not his?" I grimaced.

"There's plenty more if you're thirsty?" She offered, opening a cupboard behind her to reveal bottle after bottle of urine, all labelled with dates and notes saying things like...

"Pre apocalypse"

"Post apocalypse"

"First of the morning – Down in one"

If ever two people were made for each other, it's this pair of crazies.

Emily entered the kitchen and handed me a hot cup of black coffee. Whilst we had no electricity, we still had gas and running water.

"Here you go Dad, this will wake you up," she said.

She was smiling but her eyes told a different story. Sensing my concern she gave me a tight hug, attempting to re-assure me she was alright.

"I'm fine Dad, really. I just need to be getting on with things. We've got a lot of work to do." She smiled.

"That's right we have," Butty interrupted, beginning to swagger around the kitchen. "I think we can all agree that Skywatcher has done a tremendous job securing her house. But if we're going to survive and survive well, there's a lot more we need to do. Firstly, we need to do what Skywatcher has done to her home, to every house in Apocalypse Street, but not before we make sure for certain that each one is zombie free."

"What if we find other survivors? It's possible some of the houses might still be occupied. There might be people hiding out quietly, trying not to draw attention to themselves," Nick said.

"If we find any survivors then they can join us. Unless they're a nutter then they can fuck off," Butty responded.

I'm not sure how my brother classifies someone as being a nutter but if he's using himself as a benchmark then we could have a street filled with Arkham Asylum inmates and he'd see it as normal.

Butty continued to explain his plan to fortify the street. Explaining how once we had checked out each house we then needed to head out for supplies so we could safely secure the rest of the street and keep zombies out.

"Skywatcher, Emily and Nick will keep things running here. To make Apocalypse Street safe we need to build a wall. A wall so big and strong that a large horde couldn't break through. There's a timber yard not far from Runcorn Old Town. It's a bit of a trek but perfect for our needs. John and Dave will come with me to get supplies," he continued.

"How are going to get there?" I asked. "We could use the car but we'd need something bigger to bring supplies back."

"You'll see little brother, you'll see." The crazy bastard grinned. "But first you need to finish your coffee and tool up. We're going door to door."
?

Billy No Mates

"They should be back by now," Billy fretted, helping himself to another large brandy from the bar inside the Pavilions.

It was morning and Billy had spent the night alone after following Ged's orders to stay put whilst he and Kitty went in search of the others. Nobody had returned and he was worried.

Holding a filthy beer cloth to his mouth and nose, he reluctantly walked to the main doors of the Pavilions, hesitating for a second before pushing them open. The vinegar heavy smell from the stained beer cloth was a welcome scent compared to the stench oozing from the hundreds of zombie corpses that lay dead on the surrounding fields.

Coating the fields, a heavy mist lingered, hiding the massacred rotters from sight. Still, Billy knew they were there. He also knew they were dead but it did nothing to ease the sense of trepidation and foreboding. He had been left alone, abandoned by those he trusted.

"Come on Ged, don't leave me here alone. What the hell am I going to do?" he said anxiously to himself.

Working for Ged was all that Billy had ever known. He was the youngest of the gang and his boss had taken him in from the streets as a young stray, then quickly put to work dealing drugs, walking the streets, pushing cocaine and pills in broad daylight; his cheeky smile and innocent demeanour meant his dealing went unnoticed.

As a child, Billy was unaware of his criminal actions. All he knew was that people gave him money in return for packages and as long as he did as Ged instructed, there would be a hot meal and a roof over his head at the end of each day. What he lacked in intelligence he more than made up for with loyalty. He would do anything for Ged. He owed him everything.

Billy leant a large ladder against the building and climbed until he reached the roof. There he stood, assessing his surroundings. From atop of the Pavilions he could see out over much of Weston Point, including the large chemical plant close by and the surrounding streets and houses.

He looked straight ahead towards the road adjacent to The Pavilions, shading his eyes from the harsh morning sun and squinting to focus. Like the fields that surrounded him, he saw the road was also layered with deceased zombies. There was no sign of life.

"Where the hell did they come from?" he asked himself.

He climbed down the ladder and re-entered the building, walking with pace to the storage area. There he packed food and water into a rucksack then arming himself with a pool cue and a small fishing knife, he headed once again for the main entrance, stopping only to retrieve a bottle of brandy from the bar.

Stood on the steps of the Pavilions he guzzled some brandy then lit a cigarette.

"Stay here he said. Look after the loot he said. I'll be back soon he said. Ah fuck! No life and nothing but dead zombies for as far as the eye can see. I'm damned if I'm staying here and doing nothing. Ged, if I'm wrong then I'll take what's coming but if I'm right and you need my help, then well... When this thing is over I want a fucking pay rise. Here goes nothing," he nervously uttered to himself, before fearfully walking down the steps.

His legs trembled as he walked the mist covered path away from the building, past the zombie covered fields. His steps were accompanied by sizzling sounds, produced from the decomposing bodies as they thawed under the winter sun.

The further he walked the lesser the smog and the decaying corpses became more visible. Finishing his cigarette he flicked the butt towards the fields, where it landed in the open mouth of a badly battered zombie corpse. The head had been beaten so severely that the nose had caved in and both the eyes were missing, leaving only deep blackened sockets. It was as if they had been scooped out and the head hollowed on purpose. The thrown cigarette sent small veils of smoke weaving skywards, protruding from both the mouth and the eye sockets of the zombie. Billy reached into his pocket and placed the old beer cloth once again to his mouth and nose, before continuing his journey, leaving the grounds of the large sports club and turning onto the adjacent road.

The scale of destruction was far greater than he had thought. For as far as he could see slain zombies quilted the road, making it impossible to see the tarmac underneath. It was like an undead slumber party, and every zombie in Runcorn had turned up for a sleepover.

With carefully placed steps he slowly moved forward, eyes wide and alert for any zombies that had survived the massacre. The sizzling from the thawing dead was so loud and vast it felt to Billy like popping candy had been poured into his ears. It was becoming unbearable. So to combat the noise, he ripped the beer cloth into two pieces and twisted them into his ears. Dealing with the smell of the dead rather than listening to them was the lesser of the two evils.

He continued to move over the zombie obstacle course, sluggishly walking along the road. Then something bright shone into eyes, blinding his vision. He lifted a hand to shade his view then he saw where it was coming from. The sun was reflecting from a wing mirror of a motorbike. It was Billy's motorbike. The one that Ged had taken a day earlier.

?

Journal Entry 2

Whilst Emily stayed with Nick and the girls and Skywatcher butchered dead zombies for camouflage, 80s Dave, Butty and I went from house to house, looking for any survivors or supplies and to make sure Apocalypse Street was free from dead fucks. We'd decided to go from garden to garden rather than walk the street and move from door to door. 'More covert' was my brother's words but let me tell you something. There is nothing covert about an out of shape mayonnaise tester, a chain smoking denim clad lazy arse and a man wearing tight pants and homemade armour attempting to climb over a 6ft garden fence.

"Who's going first then?" I asked; the three of us standing in a line to the side of Skywatcher's garden, looking at the large fence that separated her property from her neighbours.

Butty turned his head to glance at Skywatcher who was looking on from her workstation, happily slicing and dicing up zombie limbs. She returned his gaze then seductively wiped blood from her face. If this was a cartoon then steam would have blown out of my brother's ears and his heart would be beating out of his chest. He turned away from Skywatcher and looked back at the wall.

"I'll go first. I'll assess the situation and give you the all clear if it's safe to come over," he informed, puffing out his chest.

"Hey hang on, ace. What if I wanted to go first? You always get to do the cool heroic shit. Maybe just this time I want to have a go." Dave asked, a tone of hurt to his voice.

"Well do you?" Butty asked.

"Nah fuck that. Only a dickhead would volunteer to go first. I'll hang back here with John till you tell us it's safe and if we don't hear from you in two minutes we'll assume you're dead and go from door to door instead. After a few seconds grieving of course. I'm not completely heartless." Dave quipped.

Butty, as always, ignored Dave's piss taking and with cat like agility jumped over the wall in one fluid movement.

"Pretty impressive that kid. Hey do you reckon if he does die I can have all his ciggies?" Dave said, asking what I'm convinced was a serious question.

"No you can get fucked!" came Butty's response from beyond the wall. "We're all clear, come on over."

"After you ace," Dave politely offered. "I'll give you a bunk up and push you over. We both know your crap back will give in if you try anything like what Butty just did. Come on then brittle bones, on three."

Dave knelt down in front of the fence and instructed me to climb up on his back and after a count of three he lifted his body up with such force that he propelled me skywards and I cleared the fence completely. Thankfully a large bush broke my fall.

Butty pulled me to my feet and for a moment he looked impressed, under the impression I had cleared the wall on my own.

"Very good little brother. Maybe there's hope for you yet," he said with approval.

I was going to tell him that Dave gave me a boost but... Hang on who I am kidding. Let's face it I was never going to tell him. It was nice getting some praise for a change.

I looked around. Whoever had lived here had green fingers and took pride in their garden. It was immaculate. There was a small fish pond, a vegetable patch, a shed and a large conservatory to the back of the house. As I admired the garden I felt something fly between myself and Butty, just missing our heads. It was the Battle Paddle. Dave had launched it over the fence like a spear, gliding between us and spiking the ground.

"Look out!" Dave shouted from behind the fence.

"You were supposed to shout that before you threw you it, dick head! You nearly had my ear off!" I yelled.

"You're alright aren't you? Quit your whining and clear the way, I'm coming over," Dave replied.

Sensing that this wasn't going to be pretty, Butty and I moved a safe distance from the fence and it's a good job that we did because instead of coming over the fence, Dave came crashing through it! There he stood with a ciggie in his mouth and a Dave shaped hole in the fence behind him. He took a drag on his tab then casually walked forward, pulling the Battle Paddle from out of the grass.

"Tell your bird she needs to get that fence looked at. Rotten as fuck lar, I'm surprised it's lasted as long as it has," he swaggered.

"Nothing to do with you being too heavy to get over it then?" I smirked.

"Me? Heavy? Piss off. My body is a temple. I'm all muscle me, ace," he replied, sucking in his gut. "Definitely a rotten fence. We can get some extra wood when we go out to get supplies for fortifying Electric Avenue. Can't we Butty lad?"

"Why do you keep calling it Electric Avenue? We've named our new home Apocalypse Street?" Butty asked.

"Well there are two answers to that question. The first is because 'we' never named it Apocalypse Street, you did and let's be honest, it's a shite name. It sounds like the name for a fucking day time soap opera. So I thought, if we're renaming streets willy fucking nilly, then I'm calling it Electric Avenue, after the hit 80s song of the same name by the awesome Eddie Grant. In fact, I'm going to rename every street in this god forsaken town after awesome 80s tunes. The street next door? I'm calling it Alphabet Street…"

Cutting Dave off was a loud whistle and we turned to see Skywalker atop of a ladder against her house. She had a severed arm in her hand, waving it about to grab our attention. It quickly became apparent what she was warning us about. From the side of the house an old man appeared. He was wearing wellies and loosely carrying garden sheers. Both handles were taken in each of his hands. He was snapping the sheers together whilst a thick drool dripped from his mouth. Oh and he was undead. I almost forget to write that as it seems everyone we meet is undead these days.

"That's Ed, it's his house." Skywatcher yelled. "It's the first I've seen of him, I didn't think he was home. He's a lovely fella."

"Oh well then, we'll invite Ed in for tea and biscuits and a natter shall we?" I replied with agitation.

The old man shuffled closer, snapping the sheers open and closed over and over. I looked around and found a garden rake lying next to the vegetable patch. Without thinking I launched the rake towards the zombie but my aim was way off. Instead of hitting the old fella it smashed through the conservatory window.

"A blind man has a better aim than you." Butty frowned whilst shaking his head.

The noise of breaking glass distracted Ed Sheer-an (see what I did there? Don't tut, it took me ages to think of that) and he turned around, shuffling towards the conservatory. We watched as he approached the broken window, groaned loudly then turned back around to face us, snapping his sheers ferociously as he began to stagger forwards.

"I think he's pissed you broke his window, ace," Dave said, finishing his cigarette.

Dave walked towards Ed Sheer-an purposefully and swung the Battle Paddle hard, giving Ed a brutal uppercut so powerful it sent his false teeth flying from his mouth. The zombie stumbled backwards before falling through the broken conservatory window.

Butty picked up the false teeth, washed them in the pond then placed them in his pocket. He looked at Dave and I, expecting to be questioned on his actions but neither of us said anything.

"You're wondering why I've taken his false teeth aren't you?" he asked.

"No, not really. I've seen you drink beer made from cheese and wear a lampshade around your neck. Nothing you do surprises me anymore,' I replied, following Dave towards the conservatory.

Head like a Hole

Nick smiled as he watched Sophie playing peekaboo with her baby sister, sat on the living room floor of Skywatcher's house. She would lift a cushion to her face slowly, whilst Gaby appeared confused as to where her sister had gone. Then she would lower it quickly, and Gaby would laugh hysterically. With everything Sophie had been through since the outbreak, it made him happy to see her play and find time to simply be a little girl. Gaby's laughter was infectious and Nick couldn't help but join in, giggling along happily, until his hangover started to kick in, bringing alcoholic sweats and dizziness.

He jadedly left the living room and stumbled down the hallway. It was dark, with the only light coming from thin sun beams, shooting through gaps between wooden boards which secured the windows. Either side of the hallway rested weaponry. Garden tools, such as spades, rakes and shovels leant against the walls next to cricket and baseball bats, saws, hammers and large knives. Skywatcher's house, although perfectly kitted out for survival, was not a safe place for children.

He entered the kitchen and poured himself a large glass of water, guzzling it down like he hadn't drank for a week. It wasn't till he'd finished and returned to the sink for a refill that he noticed Emily preparing food. A bottle of baby formula for Gaby and porridge for Sophie, mixed with water and powdered milk.

"It's almost therapeutic, doing something normal. It's only been a week and it feels like things have been this way forever. It's amazing how quickly we can adapt and even forget about how things used to be. Plus, it makes a nice change from killing zombies," Emily said, shaking the bottle of baby formula.

Also shaking was Nick's hands. They trembled uncontrollably as days of solid drinking began to take its toll. He placed them in his pockets, hoping in vain that Emily would not notice. The look on her face told him she had.

"Looks like I picked the wrong time to quit drinking. I'm fine, really. Just a bad case of the shakes. I promised Sophie I wouldn't drink anymore. Now for the first time since this all started I'm sobering up and my head feels like it's been hit by a fucking truck!" he said before stumbling to the side, placing a hand on the wall to steady himself.

Emily refilled Nick's glass and handed it to him. He again, guzzled the water without pause.

"Thanks," he gasped, catching his breath. "Apart from Jack Daniels, that's the first thing I've drank in days."

Then Nick broke down, collapsing to the floor, shaking and crying into his hands as tears rolled down his cheeks. Emily had no idea what to do. Zombies? Piece of cake! But a grown man breaking down before her eyes?

Doubtfully she moved in close to Nick, tapping her hand on his shoulder for comfort but it did not feel right. She went in for a hug but withdrew at the last minute. She patted him gently on the head but his whaling increased. So she did the only thing she knew would work. She punched him hard in the face.

Immediately Nick stopped crying and he looked at Emily with shock, blood trickling from his nose into his mouth.

"What did you do that for?" he asked.

The kitchen door opened and from the garden, Skywatcher appeared, wearing a blood soaked plastic mac and carrying an axe.

"Everything alright?" Skywatcher asked with suspicion, "I thought I heard someone blubbing?"

Nick lowered his head to hide his blood shot eyes.

"It was Sophie," Emily answered. "She was upset about her family but she's OK now. We're making her and her sister some breakfast. Do you want anything?"

"No time to eat. Got more house camouflage to make. I'm stocking up the outhouse with fresh limbs. Nick, there are tablets in the cupboard, they'll help with your hangover and if you want to cry go and do it in a corner quietly. Noise like that will attract unwanted attention," she said, closing the door and returning to her butchering.

Nick wiped the tears from his eyes and the blood from his nose and stood, brushing himself down in an attempt to pull himself together.

"Sorry about that," he said embarrassedly. "I feel so overwhelmed. Staying drunk kept my emotions in check. I just got on with it. Killing zombies and drinking booze went hand in hand. Now I'm sober, I don't know what do. I've lost so much," Nick stuttered.

"We are all the same. Everyone here and everyone you will ever meet from now on has lost someone or something they care about. You're not alone, so don't feel like you need to go through this on your own. Here, take these and go be Uncle Nick to those kids. Don't let them see that you've been crying," Emily said, pushing a bottle of formula and a bowl of porridge into his hands.

Nick's lips gave a thin smile and he walked back out into the hallway. Emily sat upon a kitchen unit and placed her head in her hands.

"I'm fifteen years old and counselling a grown man on his grief and alcohol dependency. Like I haven't got my own shit to deal with. Give me zombies to kill anyway!"

She felt tense and from out in the garden she heard the thwacking, whacking and chopping from Skywatcher as she continued to prepare camouflage for the house. Taking her rage out on the undead was exactly what she needed.

Journal Entry 3

Dave and I poked our heads through the broken conservatory window. Ed Sheer-an was writhing around on the floor, unable to get to his feet. Shards of glass ripped through his rotting skin with ease and to my surprise he was still holding on to the garden shears, snapping them open and closed. On his arm was a deep bite mark. He had been attacked, infected and turned.

"Look at him, ace. Clinging on to the one thing he loved more than anything. Gardening. And you wrecked it by destroying his conservatory. I bet you feel like shit now don't you, John?' Dave asked.

Then Dave drilled the Battle Paddle into Ed's head.

"I don't know how you can live with yourself," he added.

"We could board this up maybe. Use some of the broken fence panels but at the moment we shouldn't consider occupying this property. We'd be too exposed if we came under attack." Butty assessed, joining us at the house. "Let's have a quick scan for supplies then we'll move on to the next house. Try not to break anything else little brother."

Prick!

We entered the house. It was the polar opposite to the immaculate garden. The conservatory was being used more as a shed, housing dirty old plant pots, watering cans, garden tools and half used bags of compost. The conservatory led into a living area. All that was there, apart from piles of rubbish bags, was a deck chair and an old television set. Ed had put everything into his garden and neglected every other aspect of his life. It was no wonder that even after death he still clung on to the one thing he loved, snapping his garden shears open and closed. But this begged a question.

"Look at this house, it's so sad. It's like looking into Dave's future," I said.

"Hey old up lar. I'd have something better than a deck chair to sit on. Probably some kind of awesome recliner with a built in tape deck and cigarette dispenser." Dave remarked.

"Everything this guy cared about was outside in his garden and what do you think about those shears? I'm sure he was trying to use them. Maybe he was remembering how much he loved gardening and that's why he kept snapping them together? What if zombies are somehow beginning to remember things from their lives?" I asked.

"It's possible. In Dawn of the Dead you could say the zombies went to the shopping mall because they remembered. You could be right little brother. Let's keep an eye out for any suspicious looking zombies," Butty said.

"Suspicious looking zombies?" Dave laughed. "What, you mean like, dead fucks hanging around street corners looking a bit shifty and avoiding eye contact? Suspicious looking zombies. Good one Butty lad, proper made me giggle that did."

"John, you and laughing boy have a look around here for anything that might be useful. I'll check out the kitchen for any food," Butty instructed.

Whilst Butty disappeared into the kitchen I had a scan of the living room. Apart from the old television and deck chair, the room was wall to wall with bags of rubbish. I didn't know where to start but Dave dove straight in, flinging rubbish left, right and centre. In doing so he revealed an old dusty cabinet, hidden behind a pile of bags.

"Jackpot!" Dave grinned. "These old fellas lar. They all have a cabinet like this. Somewhere for them to hideaway the good stuff."

I automatically assumed he was talking about alcohol but then he opened the cabinet and retrieved an old metal tin. He looked at me with a beaming smile that took up his whole face.

"Batteries!" he grinned.

"Batteries? You're excited about batteries?" I asked with confusion. By the look on his face you'd think we'd struck gold.

"Fucking right I am, ace," he replied, opening the tin. "My Walkman won't power itself kid. Old people love batteries. They can't get enough of them. Every old person I've known always horded batteries, light bulbs and fucking fuses. There's enough in here to keep me going for weeks!"

We heard a 'thud' coming from upstairs.

"Could be nothing," I said hopefully. "A cat maybe?"

Then we heard another 'thud' followed by a loud throaty groan.

"That's some fucking cat," Dave replied.

Butty reappeared from the kitchen with a carrier bag containing a few tins of rice pudding.

"This is all he had in. It's not spam but the shelf life is good," he informed.

Another groan was heard from upstairs followed by the clattering and banging of something falling down the stairs. We all looked to the partly closed door which lead out to the hallway.

"What do you reckon, Butty? You're bro thinks it's a cat?" Dave said, filling his pockets with batteries.

The door opened and from the hallway shuffled undead Mrs Ed Sheer-an. She was wearing a nightgown and had dried blood around her thin, gaunt mouth. I realised then that Mrs Sheer-an must have turned first, attacking Mr Sheer-an, biting his neck and infecting him.

Butty flipped a tin of rice pudding in his hand then launched it at her head. The tin spun through the air before connecting with her forehead, busting her skull and killing her instantly. It was a superb shot. He walked over to Mrs Sheer-an and pulled the tin out of her forehead. Using her nightdress he wiped the tin clean from blood and placed it back in the carrier bag with the other tins.

"Rice pudding: tasty and deadly. Come on, lets drop these off with Skywatcher then we'll move to the next house," Butty instructed, swaggering away like Chuck Norris walking away from an explosion.

Emily & Skywatcher

Skywatcher brought an axe down fast and hard, chopping through the waist of an already arm and legless zombie.

"Need some help?" Emily asked, stepping out of the kitchen door and entering the garden, carrying two cups of tea.

The garden was well maintained, apart from the broken fence caused by 80s Dave. Flower beds boarded a perfectly cut lawn and towards the bottom of the garden was a paved seating area overlooking a large fish pond. It was beautiful and in stark contrast to the 'workshop' Skywatcher had created directly outside the backdoor of her house.

Throwing the separated zombie onto a small pile of limbs, Skywatcher nodded towards a small heap of corpses. Steam rose from it like a fresh mound of compost. Emily walked to the pile of rotters and dragged a zombie over to Skywatcher's butchering area. Picking up a spare axe she hacked at the body brutally, making short work of chopping it into pieces. Skywatcher smiled with approval.

"You've done this before?" Skywatcher asked.

"No. But this is easy," Emily replied, throwing the zombie's head onto the pile of sliced and diced up body parts. "All I have to do is imagine this is the bastard that killed my boyfriend and burnt down my uncle's house and I could do this all day. This is a pretty good stress reliever actually."

"Post-apocalyptic therapy. Maybe I could charge. Stressed out about the end of the world and watching your loved ones be eaten by zombies? Come see Dr Skywatcher and hack your worries away." Skywatcher replied in a terrible American accent.

Emily paused her chopping and glared at Skywatcher, who began to sense that her little joke might have been in bad taste.

"Oh, I'm sorry Emily. Sometimes I don't think before I open my mouth," she said apologetically.

Emily glared at Skywatcher, her face like stone. Then she burst into laughter.

"Ha ha, you should see your face," she laughed. "Don't worry I'm not offended. I actually thought it was quite funny and you're right. Chopping up zombies. It's the perfect therapy. Look at me. I'm feeling better already!"

"I think I'll leave you to it and try to fix the broken fence," Skywatcher replied, walking towards the bottom of the garden.

Emily followed. "Wait up, I'll help too. We'll get done quicker together," she said, following Skywatcher.

They both picked up the knocked down panel.

"You know you don't act like a teenager," Skywatcher said. "I was expecting you to be different. Less capable than you are."

"Uncle Butty has trained me well. My mum died when I was born. My dad and uncle raised me. Dad raised me to be polite, honest and kind. And Uncle Butty raised me to bash zombies' brains in. What about you?" Emily asked.

"Not much to tell I'm afraid. I lived here with my mum and dad and younger brother. Lived here all my life," Skywatcher replied, looking towards her house with pride.

"What happened to your family? Zombies? Did you have to...?" Emily asked.

"Yeah, all three of them. First my little brother then my parents. I had to kill them all. Hardest thing I've ever done," Skywatcher informed sadly, still looking out towards her house.

Emily placed a hand on Skywatcher's shoulder. "Sorry you had to go through that," she said.

"Oh it's alright, don't feel sorry for me. We've all been through so much. Besides. They're still here. Up there nailed to the house. They were the first bit of camouflage I used. My dad's looking a bit weathered though. Not sure how much longer he'll last," Skywatcher said, pointing to a rotting old zombie head nailed underneath the bathroom window.

Emily looked at Skywatcher's father, just in time to see his jaw fall off.

Journal Entry 4

Four houses done with three to go and we hadn't encountered any more zombies since poor old Ed-Sheeran. They had all been empty and mostly short on supplies. Every house looked like the owners had left in a hurry; taking as much food and clothes as they could. They were trying to outrun the outbreak I suppose. Maybe some of them made it. I'd like to think so anyway. Maybe some of them got away and were picked up by the army. Maybe there's a camp or even multiple camps where the human race is rebuilding. Kicking zombie arse. Or maybe their attempts at escape were futile and they're all dead or even worse, undead. I'm learning to keep my thoughts on this to myself. Whenever I bring up the possibility that there might be places secure for us to go, Butty shoots me down almost immediately. As for 80s Dave, well... I told him my theory that there must be somewhere safe, run by the military for us to go and do you know what he said?

"Military run camps for survivors? Doubt it lar? I reckon the army were given orders early on to shoot anything that moves. Dead or alive, ace. If it moves, shoot the fucker. There's not a chance the government would round up survivors, not when trying to contain the outbreak. And anyway, how shit does a survivors camp sound? I'd rather go on holiday to Butlins and last time I did that I caught herpes off a dinner plate. Don't ask."

And do you know what? I didn't ask!

With all the houses either side of Skywatcher's home cleared, we took to walking the street, going from door to door to search what remained. We had been at it all morning and Dave's belly was rumbling.

"Fucking starving I am, ace," Dave complained as we approached a door of another house. "Hey Butty, are we going to break for lunch or what? I'm running on empty. Hank Marvin, in need of some scran, gegging for munchies, lar! If I was from another country I'd be from Hungary. I'd be a hungry Hungarian. Oh for fuck's sake, now look what's happened. I can't even make funny jokes anymore. It's the hunger pains. It's taken my hilarity away!"

Butty, with his head pushed against the front window of the house, looking inside, reached into his utility belt and pulled out a cigarette case, tossing it to Dave.

"Get one of those down you and stop moaning. We'll be done soon then you can get something to eat before we head out again," he said.

"Butty," Dave began, looking at the cigarette case in his hand. "If smoking tabs filled me up I'd be the size of a house, kid. It's food I'm after, not bifters!"

Butty called for Dave to open the case and this time he did as instructed. A mixed look of surprise and confusion filled his face as he looked inside. A bit like when you try for a cheeky fart and some poo slips out.

"Pass them around but only take one each. We should start rationing what we have." Butty added, still looking through the front window.

"What the fuck is this?" Dave asked with confusion, showing the content of the cigarette case to Butty and I.

Inside the case were twenty thin strips of Spam.

"Spam sticks," Butty replied. "They are a healthy snack, filled with nutritional porky goodness. Take one and pass the tin on to John. They'll keep us going to till lunch."

Dave took a Spam stick and dangled it in front his face, examining it closely. I could see a big chunk of tobacco stuck to the porky slice and Dave moved it closer to his mouth, ready to take a bite.

"Oh Butty you could have cleaned the tin out first. There's a big piece of tobacco stuck to Dave's Spam stick," I grumbled, scrunching up my noise in disgust.

"Is there?" Dave asked, taking another look at his snack. "Get in lar!" He grinned before shoving the whole thing in his mouth in one go. "Good idea Butty lad. You've combined my two favourite things. Smoking and filling my face. Here you go Johnny boy, get one down you. It's nicer than it looks."

Dave tossed the Spam sticks over and I immediately handed them to my brother.

"I'll pass thanks. Don't want to spoil my dinner." I responded as I watched Butty suck one into his mouth like a piece of porky spaghetti.

Butty moved away from the front window and prised the house door open with a crowbar, giving us access. The first thing I noticed was the walls of the hallway. They had been painted bright pink. It was so bad it was making my eyes hurt. We moved into the living room and everything was also pink. Pink walls, Pink furniture, pink carpet, pink cushions, pink...well, you get the idea. On shelves and hanging from walls were dozens of framed photographs and canvas prints, all of the same woman in various exotic locations, wearing skimpy outfits and bikinis, pouting and posing for the camera. She was pretty. I think. Well, she would have been if it wasn't for the fake tan, bleached hair, buckets of make-up, painted on eyebrows and Botox. It was clear that the woman in the photographs was the owner of the house and she quite obviously thought very highly of her appearance. Much to 80s Dave's amusement.

"Check out Selfie Sally. There must be fifty pictures here and she's in every single one of them. Not fucking one of anyone else. Talk about self-obsessed, kid. And look at those eye brows! They look like two strips of gaffer tape stuck above her eyes." Dave laughed. "Why do women do that to themselves? Is looking like a pantomime dame all the rage nowadays or what? I've seen clowns with better eyebrows and look at that tan! She looks like she's been dipped in gravy. Must be sprayed on that lar."

Whilst Dave pondered why someone would tan themselves darker than someone entering a body building competition and draw on eye brows thicker than double yellow lines, Butty had wandered off to explore more of the house. It was only when Dave finished talking we heard him shout from another room.

"Boys! Come and have a look at this!"

We walked the hallway, finding an open door leading to an extension built to the back of the house. Dave and I entered. It was dark with the only window covered by closed blinds. But even through the darkness we could see the extension had been kitted out as a tanning salon, complete with fake palm trees, golden sand coloured walls and a bright blue sky ceiling. It was a tropical paradise. Directly ahead of us, pushed against the far wall was a large sunbed with the top down.

"Very nice but why the urgency Butty lad? Do you need help getting out of those skinny jeans so you can work on your tan? Hey, he's changed since this Skywatcher appeared on the scene don't you think so, John? Yesterday he was all about covering himself in zombie splodge, twatting dead fucks and drinking his own piss. Now he wants a tan. He'll be brushing his teeth next," Dave quipped.

A hideous and vile smell filled my nostrils, not like anything I had ever smelt before and as you can imagine, my nose has sniffed some pretty nasty whiffs these last few days. Nothing like this though. The only way I can describe it is like burnt puke and the stench hit me like a punch to the face.

"Oh Jesus, what the hell is that smell?" I gagged, pushing my shirt up over my mouth.

I moved around the room trying to find where the smell was coming from, feeling around in the darkness. I was fully expecting to find a fridge or freezer, loaded with defrosted food that had gone bad since the power went out. Dave and Butty just stood there, watching as I gagged and heaved my way around the room.

"Are you two going to help or just stand and watch?" I retched.

"I would help but it's far too much fun watching you trying to figure this out," my brother smiled.

"I'm with Butty, ace. Plus you know I've got no sense of smell so I'm not bothered," Dave added.

I moved over to the window and pulled the draw string, opening the blinds. The room flooded with light, illuminating the tropical paradise of the home owner's tanning salon. Now I could see where the smell was coming from. Hanging out of the sunbed was an arm and a leg, both blackened and burnt to a crisp.

"I reckon she's had a bit more than the recommended two minutes, lar." Dave remarked.

Butty, removing the cigarette case from his utility belt, placed a Spam stick in his mouth like it was a cigar then walked towards the sunbed, inspecting it with all the swagger of a Hollywood detective.

"I've heard of things like this happening before. Looks like she's gone for her usual tanning session and the sunbed malfunctioned, trapping her inside and burning her to death. What a way to go. Fried alive," he said, chewing on his porky stick.

"Check out Columbo over here. Judging by the pictures of her all over the house she'd be happy with the colour," Dave replied, walking to the sunbed and bending down to get a closer inspection of the crispy arm. "Check it out lar. Anyone got any BBQ sauce?"

As Dave laughed at his own joke the frazzled arm sprang to life and began thrashing about inches from his face. Dave and Butty jumped back and all three of us watched from the doorway as the top of the sunbed lifted off. Selfie Sally, the owner of the house, sat up slowly; strips of her burnt skin tore from her back, sticking to the sunbed. Shakily she stood up and looked right at us; completely naked, burnt from head to toe and all of her hair was gone.

"Is she dead?" I asked, slightly embarrassed that those words actually left my mouth.

"Dead? Ace, she looks like a fucking BBQ'd sausage," Dave replied.

Then the girl groaned. Now I had no doubt she was dead. She took one step forward, placing a crispy foot heavily to the floor. The clumsy stomp made her body tremor. The resulting shake made her scorched boobs jiggle and skin from her left breast split, sending a silicone implant falling to the floor.

"Any ideas?" I asked.

No sooner had I asked the question, I heard a noise, a strange 'splodging' noise from over my shoulder. I turned to see 80s Dave with a bottle of after sun, squeezing a dollop out into the palm of his hand.

"Really Dave? We're about to be attacked by a zombie that's been burnt to a crisp and your answer is to apply after sun?" I yelled with exasperation.

I grabbed the bottle from Dave's hand and threw it in anger, not really paying attention to where it was directed. I heard a thud followed by a slurping sound and turned to see that the bottle of after sun had hit Selfie Sally in the face, getting lodged in her mouth. The zombie took a few stiff steps forward, moving its head up and down and from left to right in what appeared to be an attempt to free the bottle from its mouth. The head movement, caused the lotion inside the bottle to pour out, filling the zombie's throat and spluttering out of the sides of its mouth. The after sun spilled to the floor and Selfie Sally put another stiff foot forward straight into a splodge of the stuff. Her foot skidded out from under her and she fell backwards, hitting the floor hard and cracking her skull. The zombie died instantly.

"That's some serious fucking ninja skills, ace. Death by lotion. I love it kid." Dave smiled.

"Very impressive little brother. There's hope for you yet," Butty added taking a few bottles of fake tan and placing them in a bag.

Noticing the questionable look we were giving him, Butty huffed and puffed, clearly annoyed that he had to explain himself.

"Camouflage. Fake tan is perfect for stealthy movement at night. Why cover your skin in dirt when one application of 'Deep & Dark' will leave you blacker than Dave's lungs. Come on, let's get a move on. I'll dump the body outside whilst you two finish the sweep of this house, Then we'll head back to Skywatcher's for lunch. I want to apply some of this before we head out again this afternoon."

"Head out? Why? Where are we going?" I asked with concern and slightly miffed at how much work Butty was making us do.

Butty grabbed the burnt zombie by her legs and began pulling her towards the doorway. As she scraped along the ground, her crispy flesh separated from her body, peeling away and sticking to the floor. Man it was gross. It sounded like the crust being lifted from the top off a hot pie.

"We're going on a trip little brother." He grinned.

A View from a Garage

Billy lugged the motorbike into the workshop and pulled down the metal shutters. He had dragged his bike for almost 2 miles. Away from the zombie massacre on Sandy Lane to Greenway Road, just outside of Runcorn Old Town. Greenway Road was long, with large terraced and semi-detached houses, a few shops, a pub and at the very bottom was his destination. A mechanics garage.

He looked over the bike. The engine had been flooded with blood and small chunks of zombie.

"A good clean and a refill and I reckon you'll be good to go. Then I can get the fuck out of this hell hole. There's shit all left for me here now," Billy said to himself.

As he moved away from the bike to gather tools he heard a vehicle approach. He peered through a small gap in the metal shutters to see a battered red Mini Cooper covered in blood pull up outside and a women wearing a cape and a hulk fist stepped out. She moved over to the powered jet wash and turned it on, washing away the blood from the car.

"Hello beautiful," Billy said to himself as he watched.

From the road a small horde of zombies approached, drawn by the noise from the jet wash. Billy reached for a weapon, grabbing a nearby wrench but stopped short of leaving the garage to help.

"Wise up Billy," he said to himself. "You can't go risking your own life for a pretty girl. Even if she does have an awesome Hulk fist.

Billy returned to the gap in the metal shutters and watched as the girl noticed the approaching zombies. Taking a bottle of brandy from a compartment on her belt she drank greedily whilst Billy's throat turned dry with envy. Once she had finished drinking she opened the car door and retrieved a large blade. It looked like something from a science fiction movie. She looked at the blade; admiring the dried blood stains that coated it. Then raising it high into the air she screamed,

"Heghlu'meH QaQ jajvam!"

She ran at the small approaching horde, slicing and stabbing the heads of each rotter like they were nothing at all. In little time, every zombie was slain and she stood over their corpses victorious. Billy continued to watch as she finished cleaning her car then drove away, with 'Eye of the Tiger' booming out of the car stereo.

Billy moved away from the hole in the shutter.

"That woman scares me more than Ged. I think I'm in love!"

Billy took a step towards his bike but was stopped by the groaning of zombies. He looked back through the hole in the shutter to see a horde, twice the size of the previous gang of shufflers, heading his way. The thumping rock riffs of 'Eye of The Tiger' was drawing them to the garage. Frantically he secured all entrances and exits; knocking over heavy storage units to push them in front of the doors and shutter. He grabbed a wrench and watched through the hole as the horde shuffled off the road, onto the garage grounds.

Billy watched the zombies as they moved around aimlessly. Their glazed white eyes, vein filled flesh and gaunt features gave him chills. He had never faced the undead alone. He always had his gang to watch his back. But now, alone and surrounded, he had never felt fear like it and he began to sweat. The back of his neck, the top of his lip and the palm of his hands became hot and clammy. He couldn't control it. He raised a hand to wipe sweat from his face and the wrench slid from his moist hand, clattering on the ground.

"Oh fuck!" he gasped.

The noise was loud enough to alert the horde outside; their harrowing groans increasing in volume as they staggered towards the garage, slamming their corpses against the shutters. Billy was surrounded with no way out. The groans and banging on the shutters increased in volume until it was all he could hear. He placed his back against the rumbling shutters and slid down to the floor, shell shocked and in a state of complete panic. Then joining the noise of zombies came a car, growing in volume as it approached. Billy snapped out of his panic induced coma and looked again through the gap in the shutters. The girl with the Hulk fist had returned and she was running over the horde in her little red Mini Cooper.

Journal Entry 5

"Get in lar! Ever since Duran Duran made sailing cool in 1982, I've always wanted a boat!"

I stood next to Butty on the bank of Runcorn's Bridgewater Canal as Dave enthusiastically boarded the small narrow boat in front of us.

It had been a short walk from Apocalypse Street to the canal and thankfully we had managed to avoid any zombies along the way. Well I was thankful for the lack of zombies anyway. Butty and 80s Dave had looked positively disappointed. They both perked up when the canal boat came into view though. In fact, I don't think I have ever seen Dave so excited.

"This is fucking ace!" he continued, exploring the boat with the enthusiasm of a child unwrapping presents on Christmas morning. "I feel like Michael Douglas at the end of Romancing the Stone. All I need is some crocodile skin boots. Doubt I'll find any crocs in this canal though lar. Can you skin a pike?"

Whilst Dave explored the boat, Butty explained his reasoning behind choosing a canal boat and I must admit, it made great sense. Our destination was a builder's yard that sat along the banks of the canal just outside of Runcorn town centre. Travelling by canal not only gave us a direct route to our destination, it also reduced the risk of having to deal with any zombies or survivors. Plus we had a clear run with no apocalyptic carnage getting in our way. Just the clear waters of the canal.

"She's the perfect transportation little brother. My hope is that the builder's yard will have a couple of large vans we can liberate and use to bring supplies back to Apocalypse Street but at least this way, our journey there will be quite pleasant. I'll steer whilst you and Dave relax and keep warm in the cabin. I know how precious you both are. Oh and look at the name of the boat. If that's not a good omen I don't know what is." He grinned sarcastically.

On the side of the boat was the name 'Miss Emily', written in beautiful lilac with flower patterns surrounding.

"Hey lads, there's a Dead Fuck on me boat. He's a lanky bastard too!" Dave yelled.

Butty and I climbed aboard to see what he was shouting about. Trapped inside the passenger cabin was a tall male zombie, pressed up against the window pane of the door, desperately pawing the glass to get to Dave.

Butty climbed on top of the passenger cabin and removing a screwdriver from his utility belt, he nodded his head, motioning for me to open the cabin door to let the zombie out.

Dave, with battle paddle ready stood guard as I tentatively crept forward, reaching out towards the door handle, all the way keeping my eyes fixed on the tall hungry zombie inside.

"Hurry up Ace, the quicker we dispose of long man, the quicker I can be Simon Le Bon and straddle the nose of my new boat whilst we take it for a voyage down the exotic waters of the Bridgewater Canal," Dave said excitedly.

"The front of a boat is called a bow, Dave, not the nose," Butty informed.

"Whatever Captain Shit Beard, let's get this zombie twatted," came Dave's reply.

Feeling the pressure from my over excited retro friend, I pulled open the cabin door and took several steps backwards. Out stepped the zombie and he was massive, lean and tall, he towered over 80s Dave and even Butty who was stood on the cabin roof had to look up. I have never seen anyone so big in my entire life. An inch taller and he would have been a danger to air traffic!

Butty reached up and stabbed the screw driver into the back of the zombie's head killing it instantly. Dave and I looked up as the zombie towering over us began to fall forward quickly. We had nowhere to run and we both ducked down, bracing ourselves for impact.

Squelch!

Dave had ducked down whilst holding on to his battle paddle, leaving his zombie slaying weapon pointing upright. The goliath zombie had fallen directly onto it and the jagged spear head stabbed through its chest, saving us both from a squashing.

Dave gripped the paddle's handle and tossed the zombie overboard into the canal, only the expected splash never came. He looked over the side of the boat to find that the zombie had been impaled onto an upturned shopping trolley that was sticking out of the murky water. We watched as slowly the weight of the zombie tipped the shopping trolley over and they both disappeared into the canal.

"I suppose one more dead thing in the canal won't make a difference," I said.

"Butty, let's get this show on the road Ace. John, have a look inside for any supplies and I'll sit out front keeping an eye out for trouble whilst looking cool as fuck listening to the awesome 80s sounds of Duran Duran. Let's go Daddy O's," Dave grinned, straddling the front of the boat.

Butty set us off in motion whilst I looked through the cabin for anything we might need. There wasn't much but I did manage to find a few tea bags, half a jar of coffee and a few bottles of water. It was another sobering moment. Pictures of the zombie we had just killed hung on the walls and with him was what looked like his family. Possibly his wife and daughter. It reminded me how lucky I was to have Emily and also how important it was to remember that every zombie we have seen and killed once had a life they held dear. Loved ones and friends. When death is all around, killing zombies could become as normal as breathing. It's important to remember that all life is precious. Especially now when there isn't many of us left.

Just as I was getting emotional I heard singing from out on the deck. I looked out of the window to see 80s Dave, still straddling the front of the boat whilst singing 'Rio' by Duran Duran.

Closed for Business

Barry stood in the shop doorway, hands on his hips as he watched the rotting world outside. Balfour Street resembled a war zone. The dead were everywhere with mangled bodies coating the road whilst zombies shuffled along sporadically, groaning as they slowly moved without direction. Not one of the rotters had showed any interest in him. They hadn't done for a while now. The deathly stink from the dead was too powerful for them to pick up on his scent.

To his left a male zombie shuffled close, wearing running shorts and a sports vest, he was short and thin. The zombie's skin was a pale blue, frozen from the cold. Barry sighed and picked up the axe handle he had left leaning in the shop doorway. He looked at his weapon. He had owned the axe handle for as long as he had owned the shop. It was always called upon to scare off shoplifters but he had never had to use it. Not until a few days ago. Now he could barely see the colour of the wood under the blood stains.

The zombie, now only a few feet away from Barry, picked up his scent and began to move with more purpose, gnashing teeth and groaning loudly. Its new found lease of undead life was short lived as Barry whacked it over the head with the axe handle, splitting its skull wide open. It was a laboured kill. He felt nothing anymore. No remorse, no fear, nothing. He had killed so many he was now just going through the motions.

He looked down at the zombie he had just killed. Its head busted open exposing fractured skull and a rotting brain. Thick, darkened blood glooping from the wound. He looked around at the rest of the corpses and listened as they sizzled in the morning sun, a welcome change in weather was starting to thaw out their frozen bodies. He hadn't seen a living soul for almost two days, not since Butty, John and 80s Dave had left to find Emily. Two days without seeing or talking to anyone and for the first time in a long time, Barry was feeling lonely.

For 30 years Baz's Newsagents had served the community; providing a daily service for people needing milk, bread, cigarettes, cheap crisps, porn magazines and everything in between. He knew everyone in the community and everyone knew him. Whatever you needed you could always rely on Barry. Now one week into the zombie apocalypse and everyone was either dead or undead, he was beginning to think that maybe, just maybe, the days of the great British newsagents was over and he should shut up shop for good.

Barry walked back inside and turned on his radio, searching the channels for a broadcast but, like the many times he had tried before, there was nothing. He felt beaten. Like he had no purpose anymore. He had given his life to providing for people and now there were no more people left to serve. Was this it? Was this how he was to spend the rest of his days? Alone?

He turned to the medical supplies on the shelf behind him. Barry stocked a wide range of over the counter drugs. Anything from cough medicine to flu relief. He grabbed as many boxes of painkillers as he could; opening them up and emptying hundreds of tablets on the counter in front of him. He looked down at the tablets. A life once full of worth had been reduced to nothing. He felt empty. It was time for him to join the dead.

"Help me. Help me please."

Barry looked up to see a young man stood in the shop doorway, blood dripping from a badly bandaged arm.
?

Journal Entry 6

The still waters of the canal took us steadily towards Runcorn Old Town. It was proving to be an almost pleasant journey, considering the circumstances. The boat ride was so smooth and peaceful, when I closed my eyes it was easy to forget about the zombie apocalypse. Then I would open my eyes and look out of the window to see a shuffler shambling along the canal bank accompanied by Dave belting out his own version of 'Rio'.

"His name is 80s Dave and he dances on the sand,
Just like this canal twisting through the zombie land,
And with his Battle Paddle dead fucks don't stand a chance,
Oh Davey, Davey smoke some tabs you're the fucking man."

I had locked myself away in the passenger cabin but wooden framed windows and doors did little to muffle Dave's singing, or shouting as it was. Have you ever heard a tone deaf Scouser trying to sing? If the answer is no then count yourself extremely lucky. If you have then you will be feeling my pain. It's like a million finger nails being scraped down a blackboard at the same time.

To take my mind off his screeching I rummaged through draws and cabinets for anything that might come in useful. There were a few bottles of water and some dried food packets. You know, the just add boiling water types such as pasta, noodles and couscous. Not the most nutritional of meals but perfect apocalyptic grub. I also found a backpack filled with clothes and an unopened letter addressed 'To Emily'. I held the card in my hand then noticed a framed picture on the wall. The photograph was of the tall zombie Butty had killed earlier and a teenage girl, presumably his daughter. I opened the letter to find a birthday card inside. The card read,

To Emily,
Happy birthday to a wonderful daughter
You are my world
All my love
Dad
X

It hit me hard. Maybe it was the girl's name, I'm not sure but I found myself overcome with sadness. Slumped back into a chair, staring at the picture of the man and his daughter. The world had become such a cruel, evil place. The photograph and the birthday card made me consider how lucky I was to have my daughter and brother.

Then I heard a thud, followed by a scraping sound. The noise was coming from behind a small door in the cabin wall. I had assumed it was a cupboard and hadn't gotten around to checking it yet. Now I didn't want to!

Now I know what you're thinking. You're thinking exactly what I was at the time. What if it was Emily, the girl from the photograph? What if she was still alive and had been hiding from her zombie father, trapped in a cupboard all this time? It's possible right? Not everything scratching and banging against doors is a zombie?

"Hello?"

No response. Well, not vocally anyway. Just more scratching and banging. Maybe she wasn't alive after all!

As much as I wanted to ignore the noise and carry on like nothing was happening for the remainder of my time on the boat, I just couldn't. I could never live with the thought that someone was alive in there and I could have saved them.

I looked outside and considered telling the others but Dave was still in 80s dream land and Butty was steering the boat. Besides, if I told Butty there was something behind the door then one of two things would happen. He would either barricade the door making sure that whatever was behind it had no chance of escape or, and this is more likely, he would take no chances and kill it.

I reached forward and flicked the door handle before recoiling quickly to the far side of the cabin, gripping the baseball bat I had tightly. There I stayed, petrified but ready for the worst as the door creaked open ever so slightly. Then nothing. The door never moved and nothing came through. Not even a sound. I edged forwarded with caution and completely shitting myself, I reached out to pull the door open. Then, like a bolt of lightning, a huge fucking Rottweiler flung the door open and jump out, forcing me to the ground. I thought I was done for and screamed for help. I had survived zombie attacks, jumped from a burning house, was nearly murdered by a maniac that talked to a severed head and I honestly thought there and then I was going to be mauled to death by a savage dog. But the mauling never came. What did come was both a pleasant and disgusting surprise as the huge Rottweiler proceeded to lick my face with its warm, slobbery tongue.

Dave burst into the cabin with his battle paddle ready for action, only to fall about laughing when he found me being slobbered to death.

"What have I walked in on? I know you've been single for a long time lad but fuck me, even I draw the line at bestiality. Butty!" he yelled outside. "Your brother has got himself a new missus. Only she's got 4 legs and loves a belly rub."

The Rottweiler jumped off my chest and faced Dave, barking and growling at him. Dave backed off towards the cabin door.

"Alright Lassie calm the fuck down I was only playing. Sit! Sit!"

Butty entered the cabin and Dave hid behind him. I'd never seen 80s Dave like this before. Nothing ever seems to faze him yet here he was, cowering from a dog. All be it a big muscly growly one that continued to bark and show its teeth. Butty reached into his utility belt and chucked the dog a few spam sticks and like magic, she stopped growling and barking to wolf them down.

"She was just hungry." Butty smiled, chucking a few more Spam sticks then stroking the dog's head. "Where did she come from?"

"She was locked away. I heard something moving so I opened the door. I know, I know, before you say it. It could have been a zombie and I should have kept the door closed. You don't have to have a go." I replied, expecting an ear bashing but to my surprise I received quite the opposite.

"Not going to have a go, little brother. In this instance you did the right thing. A dog will be a great asset to our team, especially a beauty like this. They're loyal, intelligent and take instruction well. Basically the complete opposite to you. No John, you've done a good thing for once. Welcome to the team girl, do you need a drink?" Butty smiled, beginning to open his drinks canister for the dog to drink from.

Now we all know what he keeps in his drinks canister and it wasn't long before the dog did too. Before he had even removed the lid the dog had gotten a whiff of Butty's potent piss and started to sneeze, quickly recoiling to cower behind my legs.

"You were right about her being intelligent, ace. She's not daft enough to drink your lash juice, are you pooch," Dave laughed, moving to stroke the dog, which replied with a deep growl causing him to pull his arm back with fear. "That dog does not like me. Not one fucking bit!"

"Maybe you remind her of someone?" Butty suggested. "Someone that wasn't very nice to her?"

"Yeah but I'm fucking nice to everyone!" Dave replied.

Both Butty and I gave Dave a look of disbelief and he took himself off in a huff, outside of the cabin mumbling something about 'Stupid dogs,' and 'going for a smoke'.

For a man whose hobby is being a piss taking smart arse it was surprising to see him getting upset from being rejected by a dog!

I found a bowl and emptied one of the water bottles I'd found earlier and the dog drank it greedily.

"We'll have to get her some proper food as soon as we can. There's a shop next to the timber yard we're heading to. Maybe there'll be some dog food left. First things first though. We need to give her a name." Butty said, scratching behind the Rottweiler's ear.

You never can judge a book by its cover. I've known Butty my whole life and he still surprises me daily. I was absolutely convinced he'd either want the dog gone or he'd try to eat it. My money was on the latter yet here he was, showing it more affection than I've seen him show anyone. Well, apart from Skywatcher.

I spied a name tag attached to the dog's collar and it read, Stealth. I pointed the name out to my brother. "Why is she called Stealth?" he asked.

And then right on cue, as if to answer the question about her name, a smell worse than any rotting zombie engulfed the cabin. It was one of the worst pongs I had ever smelt. Even Butty scrunched his nose up. I opened the cabin door to let the stink out.

"I guess that answers the question about her name," I coughed. "It's her arse. She's a silent but deadly guffer. A dirty little crop duster!"

I looked at the dog and I swear she was smiling at me with pride.

From outside the cabin, just above the noise of the boat's engine, we heard a commotion in the distance.

"Oi! 2 Men and their dog! You might want to come and see this!" Dave yelled.

Closed For Business Part 2

The young man trembled and shivered as his body went into shock, both from the pain and the cold. Barry finished dressing his wound then wrapped him up in a thick blanket.

"You're in shock and probably on the verge of hyperthermia." Barry informed softly. I've cleaned up your cut. It's pretty deep but it's clean. It should heal ok as long as you look after it, change the dressing regularly. I've got plenty of bandages and some antiseptic that you can take. Here, swallow these."

Barry gave the man two painkillers and a can of cherryaid to wash them down.

"My name is Barry by the way," He smiled, placing a hand on the man's shoulder, hoping that comfort would help bring his shock under control.

"I know who you are. I used to come here for sweets and pop when I was kid." The man gasped. "I lived over the road, Number 38. But we moved to another part of town when I was a teenager. I can't believe your still here. Alive." the man said followed by a painful yelp as he adjusted himself. "My name is Chris Mould."

"Ah yes!" Barry said with recognition. "I remember you. Little Mouldy, always coming in for a ten pence mix, sherbet dib dabs and a bottle of pop. I'm surprised you've still got any teeth considering the amount of sugar you used to eat. Nice to see you're still alive son. Good job you came here when you did. Well, you're welcome to stay here for as long as you need. I'll be glad of the company if truth be known. How did you hurt yourself anyway? I can see it's not from a bite."

Chris winced again as he once more adjusted himself into a comfortable position. "Something cut me in the canal. I don't know what it was but it was sharp. You know what this town is like. People throw all sorts in the canal, it could have been anything but I had to make a move and try to find help. I need your help Barry, my friends are trapped." Chris shivered.

Barry listened as Chris told him how he and a small group of friends had tried to leave Runcorn by taking a boat along the canal. They had hoped that avoiding roads and using the canal would be the safer option but they had gotten into trouble early on and the boat had sank, leaving Chris and his friends stranded on a small sandstone island. The only way off the island was to swim across the water to the canal bank but zombies had picked up their scent, with a large horde gathering. What's more, the dead had not just stayed on the canal bank. With the smell of living flesh in their nose they were shuffling straight over the edge, into the water.

At first this didn't seem a problem. A zombie would fall and disappear into the murky canal water. But then more followed. And more and more still, all falling over the edge. A small dam had started to form, a dam made from rotting zombies. As the dam increased in size, hungry zombies were no longer falling into the water, but falling on top of the deathly pile of rotters and they were crawling across the path of twisted limbs to Chris and his friends on the small island. The zombies kept on coming and after more than a day of fighting, it was decided that one of the group would attempt an escape, lead as many of the zombies away as possible and find help. Chris had volunteered, diving into the freezing canal water but he had quickly found himself in trouble. He'd swam over something sharp; something thrown in there that did not belong. Whatever it was it had ripped into his forearm and the pain had made it difficult for him to continue. The canal bank was still littered with zombies but he had no choice, he had to get out of the cold water or he would drown. Luckily, he'd caught a break and managed to climb out of the water where there was no zombies close by. Freezing cold and with an injured arm, Chris ran has fast as he could, away from the canal to find help.

"For some reason, I don't know why, I found myself running home. Not the home where I lived but the home where I grew up. Here. To Balfour street. And I found you. Don't ask me how but I think something was guiding me, like I was meant to find you. I have no doubt that if I had not I would have died. But we have to help my friends. They're in danger. They won't survive for much longer where they are. They're cold, tired and haven't eaten for days. We need to do something. Please say you'll help."

Barry lifted himself up, cracked his knuckles and walked to the shop door. He turned the sign on the door to 'closed' then turned to Chris.

"Chris, grab a carrier bag and fill it up. Drinks, Space Raiders, chocolate, toilet rolls, take whatever you can carry. Your friends need our help. Barry's is closed for business!"

Journal Entry 7

"I'm not pissing about lads, get your arses out here fucking pronto!"

Butty and I, followed by our new canine companion, Stealth, joined Dave at the front of the boat to see what had got him so worked up. He was worked up with good reason. Our journey along the canal to this point had been fairly zombie free. There had been the odd shuffler, shambling along the canal bank but it had never been anything to worry about. Now all that had changed. We were sailing towards what appeared to be the back of a large horde, all moving in the same direction. The path on the canal bank ahead of us was full of the undead, all moaning and groaning as they stumbled into each other.

"Can we turn around?" I asked.

"Does anyone know how?" Butty replied.

"You mean you don't know? But it was your idea to take the boat in the first place. You've been steering it all this way. You're the captain!" I replied with alarm.

"Doesn't mean I know what I'm doing. I've never sailed before. It's pure luck I managed to get it going in the first place. Let's keep going, we'll be alright. We're on water and they're on land. They can't get to us," Butty replied with a tone that suggested he didn't quite believe what he was saying.

We continued along the canal; my heart pounding as we caught up with the back of the zombie horde. Stealth began to growl, glaring at the zombies on the bank. As the boat moved forward we became level with a few stragglers, struggling to join the horde ahead. I stroked Stealth's head in an effort to calm her down. If only there was someone to stroke mine!

The stragglers at the back of the horde heard the boat approaching and turned to face us before shuffling off the canal bank, falling into the water. The splash as the rotters fell into the canal alerted more of the zombies further ahead and they began to turn, walking off the canal bank into the murky waters. Butty turned off the engine, both to slow us down and to make less noise but it was too late. As more zombies fell into the water the more noise they made, causing even more to follow. It was creating a domino effect of synchronised zombie belly flops as one by one zombies fell into the canal.

Now I don't think any of us up to this point had considered what happens to zombies in water. Do they float? Sink? Drown? Well I can now confirm that fuck all happens to them and they just keep coming. Single minded in their pursuit of human flesh. Some thrashed about in the water and some disappeared under, trampled on by the others but most were finding their feet and slowly moving towards us.

"They are getting closer!" Dave shouted, stabbing his Battle Paddle into the heads of any that got too close to the boat. "We need to come up with a plan and quick!"

With the boat drifting forward and zombies throwing themselves off the embankment to our right, Butty began steering the boat to our left, to a sandstone wall and beyond it, a steep hill overgrown with weeds, brambles and trees.

"Over there, look!" Butty pointed towards a tree stump, throwing the mooring rope at me. "Throw the rope. Wrap it around the stump so we can stop this thing."

"And hurry up lar! As much fun as it is playing Whac-A-Mole with zombies, this is getting intense!" Dave added, thwacking the Battle Paddle into the heads of more dead fucks as they bobbed up and down in the water, arms reaching out to grab at him.

No pressure there then! As the boat slowly moved towards the stump, I readied myself then threw it towards the target. Well I thought I had anyway. But right at the last minute, before the rope left my hand, my arm had a massive spasm and the rope ended up in the water, wrapped around a zombie's head like a noose. I swear my body works against me.

"Knob head!" Butty rightly insulted me.

With the boat moving past the tree stump and no mooring rope to stop us, we all felt lost. With more and more zombies falling into the water we had no idea how we were going to get off. Then right at that moment, Stealth walked to the edge of the boat and casually jumped onto the sandstone wall. Then she began barking at us. Now if I could speak dog I'm sure she was saying "Jump you stupid humans!"

We followed Stealth's lead and jumped from the boat. First myself, then Butty and lastly Dave, who was enjoying playing zombie Whac-A-Mole a little too much. I watched as the boat slowly sailed along the canal, towards the zombie horde ahead and more and more of the rotters walked off the path into the murky waters.

"I think that dog has got more brains than you two put together," Dave quipped.

"The only option we've got is to climb the hill. There's an expressway up there, we'll look for a car so we can get back on track and pick up supplies. Plus we'll get a clear view of the canal up ahead and see what's got all these zombies so excited. Come on," Butty instructed before starting the steep climb.

The hill, covered in bushes and brambles was a difficult climb. With every step taken our feet got tangled in branches, making progress slow going. Apart from Stealth that is. She was having a great time, Bounding about with abandon making easy work of the climb. She must have been locked up for a few days at least and was now making the most of her freedom. She must have been dying to get off the boat and have a run about. The other thing she was dying for was a massive shit and I haven't laughed much since the world ended. As you can guess, I've not had much reason to but even when making a difficult climb with a canal full of zombies below us, watching 80s Dave be halted in his tracks by a large Rottweiler squatting in front of his head to curl out the biggest Mr Whippy shaped poo you have ever seen was enough to make my belly ache.

"Fuck me lar, like she couldn't have crimped one out anywhere else. Oh no, right in front of my fucking face. I told you she doesn't like me!" Dave complained whilst navigating his climbing around the impressive poo.

We reached the top of the hill and climbed over a small wooden fence. We were on a large expressway leading to the now destroyed Runcorn Bridge. A mixture of crashed and abandoned cars filled the road for as far as we could see. In between the cars were discarded bags, suitcases, belongings and of course, corpses. Many looked to be half eaten and ripped apart by the dead.

"Look," Butty said enthusiastically, pointing to a large truck further up the road.

We ran along the hard shoulder, moving towards the truck. The noise from the zombies on the canal below became louder the more we moved. Leaving Butty to inspect the truck Dave and I looked down the hill. We had come far enough along to see what the zombies were heading towards. Where the canal split into two channels, there was a small sandstone island and stranded on that island was a group of survivors. Maybe 5 or 6 but it was difficult to tell from our position. In the water between the island and the canal bank was what looked like a half sunken boat. The survivors were in serious trouble, surrounded by hundreds of zombies both in the water and on the canal path, with more closing in.

"Those guys are nothing short of fucked." Dave surmised. "Give them their due though, ace. Judging by the amount of floating corpses down there, they've been fighting them off for some time. Not sure how much longer they can keep going."

Dave was right. The canal was swamped with dead zombies. Those that continued to fall in, were now starting to fall on top of bodies rather than into water. That's how full it was.

"If it carries on then before you know it they'll have created a dam," Dave added. "A damn of the dead. A blockade of dead fucks. Good job we got off the boat when we did lar. Even if it does mean I can't be Simon le Bon anymore."

"Nothing we can do for them. There's on their own," said Butty, joining us to see the mayhem below. "Come on, I want to show you something."

We turned away from the horrors on the canal and began walking to the truck Butty had been inspecting. We'd only taken a couple of steps when we heard a familiar voice coming through my brothers walky talky.

Churkuh!

"Hello, Butty can you hear me? It's Barry, and if you can hear this I could do with some help. There's a copy of Splosh in it for you."

Between A Dead Fuck and a Hard Place

Barry and Chris left the newsagents and made their way through the back streets. They were making slow progress towards the canal, avoiding the main roads that connected the town. These streets, home to mostly small terraced houses, were largely quiet. There were shufflers of course but never in numbers of more than two. It was nothing that Barry and even the injured Chris couldn't handle.

"Wait here," Barry instructed as he left Chris to bash his axe handle through the head of a nearby zombie.

Chris approached and looked down at the dead zombie, its head lay busted open with thick dark blood and chunks of brain splattered on the ground.

"Have you killed many zombies?" Chris asked. "I've killed sixteen since it all began. Fifteen of those came when we got trapped on the canal. I wonder how many it takes till you stop keeping count?"

"About three hundred," Barry replied to a shocked Chris. "It was then that I stopped counting. So you've got a long way to go until you stop torturing yourself."

They moved forward at what felt like a snail's pace. Barry had patched Chris up the best he could but he was in rough shape, wincing and holding his arm as he laboriously carried on.

"You must have known a lot of them? The zombies you've had to kill?!" Chris asked. "That must have been difficult. You've had your shop for a long time. Everyone around here must have bought something from you at some point."

"Aye, that's true. A lot of familiar faces have been battered with this axe handle," Barry replied, lifting up his blood soaked weapon to look it over. "I even had to kill my own paperboy and you're right, it's not been easy, especially not at first. After a while though. All this killing, well... It all becomes a bit of a blur. Like going through the newspaper delivery orders every morning and re stocking the shelves with porno magazines. You just go into autopilot."

From out of an open door to a terraced house a male zombie shuffled. He was an older gentlemen, wearing blue overalls and underneath the blood soaked material, grease stains were visible. Barry approached and pelted the zombie in the face with the axe handle. The force of the hit was so strong that the zombie flew backwards against the living room window of the house. Blood smeared down the glass as the body fell to the floor.

"That was Mick Tolley. I went to school with him. He married Tulla Stevenson, my childhood sweetheart. Proper bell end he was. It's not nice that he's dead but I can't say I'll miss him," Barry said, wiping the blood from the axe handle on the clothes of the dead zombie.

Chris stepped forward and looked down over the battered body of Barry's former love rival.

"Like you said Chris, I knew a lot of people in this town. You've got to do what you've got to do. Stay alive long enough and everyone will have to kill someone they know. Even you. But let's hope it's not me you're having to kill though eh? Come on, we've still got a fair way to go before we reach your friends."

Apocalypse Girl pulled the severed leg out of the front left wheel of her car. Whilst running over zombies was fun and the perfect stress reliever, it was the second time in an hour she had been forced to stop and free up the wheels from mangled body parts. The car had stalled outside Runcorn train station. Somewhere she thought could be a good place to loot, knowing there was a small shop inside. But the station had already been ransacked and smashed up with several corpses on the ground outside the main entrance; both human and zombie.

In the wing mirror she spied a man on a motorbike. He was stationary, hiding behind a wall further down the road in an attempt to go undetected. She'd clocked him following her when she first stopped to free up body parts from under the wheels. She ignored him back then but now she was getting pissed off. She threw the leg down the road in the direction of the man following her and he quickly pulled himself and his bike further back behind the wall.

Apocalypse Girl walked to the other side of the car and looked at the front right wheel. Whatever body part it was that was lodged in there was so mangled it was impossible to identify. She reached in to grab it, her hands sinking into the squishy pulp. After a few seconds her hands wrapped around something that felt like bone and she began to pull but it was no good. There was no way it was budging. She needed help and against her better judgement she turned to her stalker.

"Hey arse wipe!" she yelled. "Either fuck off or come and give me a hand!"

"Fuck!" Billy sighed, placing his back against the wall.

Pissed at how bad he was at following her he now had a decision to make. Leave or join the woman with the Hulk fist and cape. Now his gang was gone he had no identity and he longed to be with people and feel part of something again. There was so much about this woman that reminded him of Ged. She was fearless and strong. Two things that he was not. Not on his own anyway. But with her he could be.

"This is your last chance dipshit! You've been following me for a reason so what's it going to be?"

He climbed onto his bike and let out a few deep breaths.

"It's now or never Billy," he said to himself. "Time to convince her you're the perfect companion. Just don't mention all the bad stuff you've done."

He revved the bike and pulled away, out from behind the wall and along the road towards Apocalypse Girl and the train station. His legs and arms were shaking. She both scared and turned him on. If he fucked this up she would probably kill him, he thought.

Bringing the bike to a stop he climbed off and walked towards her. He wanted to speak. To say something like, 'Yeah I've been following you. I wanted to make sure you weren't a psychopath and you know, maybe we can join up? Form a formidable team that can survive in this crazy world. Then after time, who knows. Maybe we will become lovers and make beautiful post- apocalyptic genital banging on top of a mountain of corpses'. But no. His throat dried up and he just stood their staring at her.

"Are you mute?" Apocalypse Girl asked before taking a long swig of brandy. "Anyway, I don't care if you can talk or not. I need you to help me with something."

She led Billy to her car and showed him the mush of skin and bone that was lodged between the wheel and the frame.

"I've tried pulling out that, err, whatever it is but it won't budge. The car won't move till it's gone. Any suggestions, mute boy?"

Billy gulped. His mouth was so dry and barren of moisture it was a difficult and painful swallow but his effort brought up enough spit to lubricate his throat.

"You need something sharp to cut it out," he croaked. "You got a knife?"

Apocalypse Girl lifted her Bat'leth to Billy's face and grinned as he turned white with fear.

"I've got this?" She smiled, enjoying seeing him squirm. "But it's too big. Good for slicing heads off though."

"There's a shop inside the station," Billy replied nervously, slowly pushing the blade away from his face. "It sold food so they'll have a kitchen. There will be something in there we can use. I'm Billy by the way."

She looked at him for a few seconds before lowering the Bat'leth and walking towards the station entrance.

"Are you not going to tell me your name?" Billy yelled.

"Nope!" Apocalypse Girl replied.

Billy was in love.

"Fucking gross!" Chris squirmed as he looked down at a rotting zombie with maggots crawling out of its mouth.

"We'll be seeing more of this," Barry replied. "A lot more. The weather is warming up and with the amount of dead in this town it's not going to take long for disease to spread. The best thing will be to burn the lot of them. Have you ever smelt burning flesh, Chris?"

"Can't say I have." Chris replied lifting his shirt over his mouth and nose as he watched a maggot wriggle out of the zombie's nose. "I singed the hairs on my arm on a gas fire once. It smelt like a bag of pork scratchings."

"I'd say that's pretty close. Now imagine burning every corpse in Runcorn. The whole town will smell like an enormous bag of hairy pork scratchings. Oh I think my tummy just rumbled. Come on Chris, not far to go now."

They walked along the once busy underpass. It was a wind trap and they both felt resistance from strong gusts as they moved. No cars passed through now and the only other things under the bridge were piles of rotting pigeons, fallen from their nests. The road above them led to the now destroyed Runcorn Bridge and once brought traffic in and out of the town. Hearing something, Barry placed a hand on Chris' chest to stop him.

"What is it? I hear nothing." Chris said.

But then, brought in on a strong wind he heard it. Groaning. An echo of what sounded like hundreds of zombies groaning together. Chris felt like he had been punched in his gut. The situation he left his friends in was bad. And now, with the canal close and the frightening sound of a hungry horde echoing all around, he was sure things had gotten a hell of a lot worse.

Apocalypse Girl stepped through the broken doors of the train station and looked inside. Ticket machines had been upturned and 2 corpses greeted her. She turned to see where Billy was and found him stood over the body of a large male which lay dead on the ground next to a taxi cab; a large hole to the back of his head.

With great effort Billy rolled Tom's body on to his back and looked upon his face. He didn't look like a zombie and appeared as if he was human when he was killed.

"Tom. Who the fuck did this to you?" Billy gasped.

He looked around. Wherever Tom was, Ed was always close by but not this time. He was nowhere to be seen. He looked to Apocalypse Girl and caught her glaring back at him.

Thud!

A rotting hand slapping against the driver's window from inside the taxi cab made Billy jump back in fright. He looked again to Apocalypse Girl who shook her head at how pathetic he was before disappearing to explore the train station.

He moved away from the taxi taking a few steps towards the station where he found the body of his friend, Deano. The back of his head was busted and cracked open and next to him was his motorbike. Billy felt numb. Like Tom, Deano appeared to have been murdered whilst he was human. This wasn't done in defence against a zombie. They had been killed in cold blood.

Stepping onto broken glass, Billy cautiously entered the train station and looked around.

"Found it!" Apocalypse Girl triumphantly yelled from out of sight.

Billy followed her voice to the station shop, clambering over the broken metal shutters that rested bent and damaged on the ground. From inside the shop kitchen, Apocalypse Girl appeared, holding a huge carving knife.

"This will do the trick. I'll carve up what's blocking the wheel then I'll be on my way. See if you can find any bags around here and fill them with as much junk food as you can. There's a lot of chocolate bars here. Just don't take any out of that guy's mouth, he looks like he enjoys a snack." She smirked, pointing the knife to the dead body of Johno, his mouth loaded with confectionary.

Upon seeing Johno, Billy's vision blurred and the room began to spin. He vomited heavily before falling to his knees. Apocalypse Girl pushed a bottle of rum under his nose.

"Takes a bit of getting used to doesn't it? I've seen a lot these last few days and I've seen all of it through drunken eyes. I don't think I've been sober since this all started. Here, drink. It makes all the death more bearable," she said.

Billy took the bottle and swigged greedily. The thought crossed his mind to tell her about Ged and the others. But he dismissed that thought as quickly as it arrived. He was only just winning her over and he didn't want to be alone again. His past, like his former gang mates, was better off dead.

They left the station, both carrying bags filled with food supplies. Taking the large carving knife, Apocalypse Girl stabbed and sliced the limb lodged between the wheel until it was free, pulling out a shredded and mangled leg. Tossing it to the road she turned to Billy.

"Those bags you've got. Keep them. They're yours. I'm not looking for company. I'm better on my own. See you around. Try not to die,' she said, climbing into her car and starting the engine.

"Wait!" Billy pleaded.

Apocalypse Girl looked at him, waiting for more but he couldn't find the words. The look on his face said it all. He didn't want to be alone.

Then the noise came, groaning from a large horde of zombies was carried in on a wind. Apocalypse Girl turned off the car engine so she could hear it clearly. She reached into the glove compartment and removed a bottle of brandy, taking a large swig. Billy looked scared. Apocalypse Girl looked excited.

"Wanna kill some zombies?" She smiled.

Journal Entry 8

"Where are you? We're on the expressway overlooking the canal and what looks like two hundred Zombies." Butty spoke into his C.B. radio.

"Take a look further along the canal, past The Brindley. Do you see that old fella with a Walky Talky in one hand and waving at you with the other? Well that's me and the lad next to me is, Chris. Those people on the little island in the water, surrounded by the dead are his friends. We're going to save them. Hopefully! We could do with some help if you're not too busy?"

Further along the canal, past the large horde and stood next to The Brindley Theatre, we could make out two figures waving at us. Despite the situation it was good to see and to hear Barry's voice again. And whilst Butty paced back and forth, talking to Barry over the airwaves, Dave and I looked on in silence. Even Stealth was being quiet. Our little trip to gather materials to fortify Apocalypse Street had so far not been unsuccessful. But now we had found a truck. A way to get the supplies we need and get the hell away from the mammoth horde of Dead Fucks. So the minute something good comes along what should happen? We get a call to arms from Barry and instead of running away from the horde, my brother had that look about him that said he were going to run in to it!

Butty lowered the C.B. from his mouth and turned to Dave and I. He had an almost apologetic look on his face.

"He was there for us when we needed him. Now he needs us. We can't leave him hanging, we just can't. Plus there's a copy of Splosh with my name on it if we do!" he said.

I couldn't believe we were going to do this again. Not two days since we battled hundreds of zombies near The Pavilions and we were about to do it again. I was really starting to miss eating mayonnaise for a living!

My brother was right though. We had to help Barry. Before, those guys trapped on the canal were strangers and in this cold hearted new world, strangers are not always worth risking your life for. Let's be fair here, we've met more than our share of crazy bastards lately. But now we know Barry is involved and that changes everything.

"So what's the plan?" I asked. "We can't exactly drive into them all like we did last time. The canal bank is too narrow for that. We'll never get the truck along there!"

Right at that point we heard music. A song we all knew echoed all around. It was Eye of the Tiger by Survivor, the awesome and inspirational song made famous by the Rocky movies. It was so loud that Dave took his headphones off!

"Can everyone hear Eye of the Tiger or have I finally gone crazy from listening to too much 80s music?" Dave asked.

"We hear it," I replied. "But where is it coming from?"

We looked down to the canal below and racing along the bank, hurtling towards the back of the horde was the source of the awesome music. A red Mini. The same red Mini, the girl with the cape and Hulk fist was driving a few days ago when she came to our rescue. We watched the car zoom forwards, hitting a few zombie stragglers, sending them flying into the water as it raced along. Then the car hit the back of the horde, sending more rotters flying through the air in every direction. Then it reversed about 200 yards and did the whole thing again.

The music and the noise of their undead brothers and sisters being victims of a hit and run, was turning the zombies' attention away from the group trapped on the small island. They were slowly turning to the red Mini.

"Ah it's her again. I think I'm in love!" Dave beamed.

"There's no way she can take them all out," I said. "Not in that battered little car. There's too many."

"I don't think she's trying to take them all out little brother." Butty smiled. "The music is turning their heads. Look, they are following the car."

He had that glint in his eye. That look that I'd come to recognise as meaning two things.

1, he had a plan,
2, I wasn't going to like it.

"You've thought of something haven't you?" I asked with trepidation.

"I have. I think we'll survive," came the reply.

Think we'll survive! He sure knows how to fill me with confidence! Then he went on to quickly explain his plan, which was dependent on two things. Getting the truck started and how deep the canal was.

Fuck!

We entered the cabin of the truck. Dave and I in the passenger seats and Butty driving. My brother set about trying to hotwire the truck; reaching under the steering wheel for wires. We entertained him for a few seconds. I think deep down he knew that we knew, he really didn't have a clue what he was doing. Then Dave pulled down the sun visor above the driver's seat and the keys fell into Butty's lap.

"Smartarse," Butty sneered.

He started the engine and off we went on our trip to certain doom! It's a short journey from the expressway into Runcorn Old Town and to the canal where the dead were waiting. But those few minutes felt like an eternity. There was a quietness in the truck, as we all geared up for a fight and thought over the half- cocked rescue plan.

Butty pulled the truck over to the side of the road, stopping just short of the turnoff that would take us to a car park and The Brindley Theatre, which overlooked the canal. About 100 yards away from the Brindley was the survivors, and the little sandstone island.

Butty talked into his C. B. radio as the loud groans from the zombies close by made the seats of the truck vibrate.

"We're here," he said.

Further up the road, Barry and his friend stepped out from behind one of the many kebab houses that make up Runcorn High Street. They quickly moved towards the truck.

Runcorn High Street was as expected. It looked like a war zone. It did before the zombie outbreak to be fair. Especially on a Saturday night when the pubs emptied. Smashed up and abandoned vehicles littered the roads and the bus station was all but destroyed.

Even the public toilet had been ripped out and upturned. Amongst the chaos, there were zombies heading towards the canal, attracted by the groans from the growing horde and of course, the epic Eye of the Tiger that could still be heard.

Barry and Chris, after taking out a few dead fucks on their way, arrived at the truck and I opened the door to let them in. It was a tight squeeze fitting them both in, with the three of us and Stealth already inside. I almost sat on Dave's lap as I tried to make room, much to his disapproval.

"Hey, watch it, kid. You've got to buy me dinner before you get to have a go on me sausage!" he barked.

"Thanks for this lads, we really appreciate your help," Barry said.

"No thanks needed Baz," Dave replied. "You've helped us in the past. It's only right we repay the favour. Just don't get us fucking killed!"

Chris reached out a hand to introduce himself and I noticed he was really struggling; holding his arm free to apply pressure to a bloodied wound. Butty noticed this too and our look of concern did not go unnoticed by Barry.

"He's hurt but it's not a bite. There's no need to worry, I give you my word. So, is this plan going to work?" Barry asked.

"It has to. It's the only plan we've got. Tell you what, we stand a better chance now the girl in the cape has turned up." Butty replied.

Barry presented a look of confusion, so we explained about the girl in the Mini with her cape and Hulk fist and how she came to our aid once before. Gradually Barry's expression changed from confusion to one of recognition.

"Ah, you mean Apocalypse Girl." Barry smiled.

Now we all looked at him with confusion!

"I'll explain when this is all over," he added.

Butty started the engine and my stomach dropped with fear. This half-baked plan to rescue these people was reckless at worst and downright ridiculous at best!

"Everyone ready?" he asked.

"No!" we all replied.

"Good. Let's do this!" he said with purpose.

Then a ghastly smell filled the cabin as Stealth puffed out a silent fart and crop dusted every single one of us.

And so, trembling in fear and with a mouth full of dog fart we headed towards the horde.

What the fuck were we doing?

DEAD TOWN

SERIES 2

The Scripts

FADE IN:

INT. AIRPLANE.

John is sat by a window. On the seat next to him is Emily's coat. On the drop down table is a little birthday cake and a birthday card.

Across from John is a man reading a book. A stewardess is seen walking the isle to the back of the plane. The man reading looks at John and smiles.

John

It's my first proper holiday with my daughter; she's just nipped the loo. She's so excited! She's never been abroad before.

Man

Aw that's nice, I hope you both have a wonderful time. She's a lucky girl to have a dad as thoughtful as you.

The stewardess approaches John.

Stewardess

We'll be serving food shortly.

The stewardess walks away and John Smiles to himself, turning to look out of the window.

With his eyes closed he turns his head away from the window, facing the man reading. He opens his eyes to see that the man has turned into a zombie.

Zombie man

You're going to die John!

John screams.

Zombie Man

But not before I've ripped your daughter to pieces ha ha ha ha ha!

John Screams.

Brittain, from episode 2 of series 1 pops his head over the seat in front, startling John.

Brittain

Hello John, are we off to see the Spice Girls?

John Screams.

The stewardess returns with a food tray containing a bloodied brain and fingers.

Stewardess

Dinner is served, hahahaha!

John screams.

80s Dave's voice can be heard over john's screams.

Dave

John, John, John!

INT. HOUSE. DAY

John wakes up with a jump, brought back to reality by Dave yelling his name. He wakes to find he is in an abandoned house with 80s Dave.

Dave

Nice that John. There I was telling you about how Phil Collins single handily changed the face of British music with his epic Sussudio and you fucking nodded off! Charming that lar.

John

Sorry Dave. What with fighting our way out of the lock up yesterday and worrying about Emily, I must have passed out with exhaustion. I've just had the worst nightmare. I dreamt I was on a plane with Emily and everyone turned into zombies. There was a brain cake...It was horrible!

Dave

Once or twice. Hey, I'll tell you what, I'm fucking starving lar. Must be all this talk of peanut pubes. What do you reckon the chances are of us finding a Greggs that's still open?

John

Greggs? It's the end of the world and you want a sausage roll?

Dave

Not just any sausage roll. A Greggs sausage roll. They are fucking delicious lar. Heaven wrapped in flaky pastry. You can't whack it kid. If I had to choose my last meal it would be a plate loaded with Greggs sausage rolls. I'm getting a little chubby just thinking about it.

John

Not for me. If I had to choose my final meal it would be something swanky and posh by a Michelin starred chef like Heston Blumentile.

Dave

Heston fucking Blumentile? Fuck that Ace. I'd rather starve than eat any of the weird shit he serves up.

John

Why what's wrong with it?

Dave

He's off his tits! Bacon dessert? Egg ice cream? Fish eyeball cocktails? He's a fucking head the ball John! No, not on my watch.

John

The only thing on your watch is a calculator pad.

Dave

Is fucking right and not once in its thirty year life has it ever lost time. Apple releasing a Smart Watch? Well I've got the original kid and it's a fucking beast! Where was I? Oh yeah, Heston Bluminshite! I have a theory as to how he makes all those weird fucked up concoctions. Have you heard of a film called The Human Centipede? It's about a freak that makes a daisy chain of people, joined together surgically mouth to arse. Well I reckon that's what goes on in Heston's kitchen. He's got his own human centipede which he force feeds any old muck and serves up what's shat out at the end!

John

He'd have to have two human centipedes because of nut allergies.

Dave

Good thinking kid. And maybe a third for vegetarians. This Heston prick is turning into a right sick bastard isn't he?

Dave hears a noise and walked to the window. Butty is outside doing a series of bizarre hand gestures at the window. John Joins Dave.

John

What the fuck's he doing?

Dave

Beats me kid. Dancing at a rave?

John

What are you going?

Butty looks frustrated then repeats the hand signals.

John (CONT'D)

Are you having a stroke?

Butty is infuriated and does the hand gestures one more time. John and Dave look at each and shake their heads.

Dave

How many syllables?

John

Is it a film or a book?

Butty marches towards the house in annoyance; opening the door and rushing up the stairs before opening entering the room to face John and Dave.

Butty

What I'm saying is that I have located a vehicle and to approach with caution and in silence!

John

Why didn't you just say that?

Butty

Because I was trying to be quiet you massive anus. Noise attracts zombies as we learnt at the lock up yesterday. Follow me and be quiet about it, I may have found us a lead in our search for Emily.

John and Dave follow Butty out of the room and down the stairs.

EXT. FRONT OF HOUSE. DAY

Butty leaves the house followed by John and then lastly, 80s Dave. Butty and John walk away whilst Dave stops outside the house to light a cigarette. A zombie appears and shuffles towards Dave who moves the peak of his cap to the side and head butts the zombie.

EXT. BACKSTREET. DAY

We see a car. It looks abandoned at first glance. John, Dave and Butty are in the distance, looking at it.

A Close up of the car. Glass and blood cover the road next the driver's door, which is open. Hanging half out of the door is a dead women. She is on her back, bent backwards with her head hanging out of the car with her arms reaching out; fingers almost touching the glass on the floor. Blood is dripping from her fingers and glass has shredded her hands. She is wearing an evening dress with a pink feather bower and an L plate around her neck.

John

May I suggest we carry on walking until we find something else?

Butty

I only see one dead person. If it's a zombie that's nothing we can't handle. Keep on your guard and follow my lead.

Butty dashes forward in full combat mode, commando rolling his way to the car.

John

Does nobody listen to anything I say around here?

Dave – Following Butty

Come on Ace, we gotta check it out. Where's your sense of adventure?

John- Staying put

I puked it up outside the mayonnaise factory right after you killed our boss.

Dave

Ah now, come on John. He was a zombie. You can't kill something that is already dead.

John

Fuck my life!

Side shot, taken from the rear running along the side of the car, showing the dead women hanging out of the open side door and the glass on the floor.

John Joins Butty and Dave at the car and puts his hands to his nose and mouth.

John (CONT'D)

Christ that smell. It's like boiled cat shit. Why isn't it bothering you two?

Butty

I've been simulating the stench of dead people at home for a long time, so that when the zombie apocalypse arrived, my sense of smell would be fully adapted.

Butty takes in a deep breath.

Butty

A job well done I'd say.

John

How did you do that?

Butty

Beef and Tomato Pot Noodle, goose fat, a large pack of parmesan cheese, 11 raw eggs, grated toe nails, clotted cream which has been opened and stored in a warm room for 3 weeks, chicken giblets, a dead ferret that's fermented in vinegar for 3 months. Then all of that is blended together with stale meatloaf, strawberry milkshake and left to fester on top of a hot radiator for several hours. The smell generated is more putrid and foul than one hundred zombies.

John, looking like he is going to puke, turns to Dave.

Dave

Don't look at me Ace. I've got a smoker's nose. I can't smell or taste anything.

John

That explains why you like Gregg's sausage rolls so much.

Butty steps forward and looks over the girl hanging out of the car.

John

What do you think happened?

Dave

Well if I had to hazard a guess Ace, I'd say it crashed.

John

I know that, double denim!

Dave

Alright narky arse, calm down. I'm only trying to put a smile on your face, there's no need to rip my awesome threads.

Butty steps back from the car and re-joins the others.

Butty

I've assessed the scene and I've deduced that what we have here is a dead woman.

Dave

Get a load of fucking Sherlock Holmes. Next you'll be telling me she was about to get married.

Close up of the 'L' plate around her neck.

Butty

How did you guess?

John

Why are we here anyway? I thought you said this had something to do with Emily? It doesn't exactly look road worthy and even if we did get it started there is no chance I'm taking a ride with a dead girl.

Dave

Necrophilia not your thing kid?

Close up of the dead girl's hand starting to twitch.

Butty

Let's see if it runs. It doesn't look too bad. A bit of tinkering and I think we'll get it started. Come on, let's shift the dead girl and see if it works.

The woman lifts her head and reaches out at the guys, gnashing her teeth whilst trying to grab at them. They quickly take a few steps back.

John

Maybe you wanna assess the scene again Butty because your dead woman is an undead women!

Butty

Now is as good a time as any little brother. She's all yours.

Butty hands John a bat.

Dave

Go on Ace, lose your zombie slaying cherry.

Reluctantly, John steps forward, readying his bat to attack the zombie bride to be.

John

I don't think I can do it.

Butty

Just remember she's not human, or even alive. She doesn't feel, she can't be reasoned with and she can't think. All she desires is one thing and that is to eat you.

Dave

Sounds like me ex.

John

I don't think I can.

Dave

Just tell yourself this. Imagine she's a reporter for The Sun newspaper and...

John steps forwarded and viciously whacks her repeatedly with the bat. Butty and Dave watch on as the attack continues and blood sprays from the zombie, covering John's shirt and face. Finally his onslaught ends.

John

That was easier than I thought.

They pull the dead zombie out of the car and Butty sits in the driver's seat. He tries the engine but it won't start.

Butty

Ah, bollocks!

John

Great, told you so. What's all this got to do with finding Emily anyway?

Butty

Nothing. Look over there little brother.

Butty motions for John to look further up the road, where a dead zombie sits slouched against a wall with a Hockey stick, sticking out of its mouth.

EXT - BACKSTREET - DAY

John, Dave and Butty are standing over the zombie with the hockey stick protruding out of its mouth.

John

That's Emily's alright. I'd recognise it anywhere.

Close up of the hockey stick with 'Property of Emily Diant' carved into it.

Dave

That's good news Johnny boy. It means she's still kicking. Not that there was any doubt.

Butty

Of course she's still Kicking. Kicking Arse.

Butty grabs the hockey stick and pulls it out of the zombie's mouth with both hands, then gives it to John.

Butty

She'll be wanting this back when we find her. Come on, the canal isn't too far away. If she's passed through here I bet that's where she's gone. No streets and Runcorn Shopping City is close by if she needs supplies. This way.

Dave

Oh hang on...

Dave rifles the zombie's pockets.

John

What are you doing?

Dave

Looking for ciggies. I'm almost out.

John

You're stealing from the dead now?

Dave

Says you, granny jacket. Yeah!

Dave pulls out a vaper cigarette from a pocket.

Dave

Oh for fuck sake. I remember a time when everyone smoked. Now they all walk around sucking down on something that looks like Dr Who's sonic fucking screwdriver. Fucking quitters.

Dave throws the vaper cigarette to the ground and begins to walk away. He stops, turns around and runs at the zombie, booting its head from its shoulders.

FADE IN:

EXT. MOTORWAY - DAY

John and Butty are walking side by side down the middle of a motorway. 80s Dave is not too far behind them. He is dancing to music pumping through his headphones.

John

Do you think the military are fighting back? Moving from city to city wiping out the hordes? Maybe once the cities are secure they'll move on to the smaller towns and we'll be saved?

Butty

Don't talk shite little brother. If the military had any kind of control over this we would have heard something by now.

John

What about that zombie soldier you said you saw? The one you killed with your slingshot?

Butty

Territorial Army, John. Nothing but a toy soldier, killed by a toy zebra. No. We're what? 3 days in to the apocalypse now? Where's the gun fire? Bombs? RAF fighter jets? We've seen or heard nothing. No, we're on our own and in this for the long haul. Me, you and dancing boy back there. Oh and Emily once we find her.

John looks dejected. Filled with sadness at the thought of his daughter.

Butty (CONT'D)

Hey, you can get that look off your face for a start. She's fine little brother. That hockey stick you're holding is all the proof we need.

John

I hope you're right Butty. I can't lose her. She's all I've got.

Butty

Oh thanks!

John

You know what I mean.

Butty

Emily, you, me, Wayne Sleep.... We are all each other has. And we will all be together very soon. Not too far to go now. A bit further then we'll...

Butty places his hand on John's chest to stop him from walking further. Something in the road ahead has caught his eye.

Butty (CONT'D)

I don't believe it.

There is a man on the road ahead. He is knelt down over a dead zombie with his hands inside its torn open stomach, removing intestines. The man is wearing a t shirt that has a picture of a UFO and the words 'Probe Magnet' underneath. His name is Mab. 80s Dave joins Butty and john.

Dave

Is that a dead fuck?

Mab removes some intestines, examining then throwing them away when he can't find what he's looking for.

Butty

No, that's not a dead fuck. That's Mab.

John

You know him?

Butty

You could say that.

Dave

What is he doing?

Butty

Looking for evidence.

John

Evidence of what? What it had for breakfast?

The man noticing the guys, throws down some intestines and picks up a large bloodied knife.

Mab

Stay back! Don't come any closer! Put your hands up where I can see them!

John

Did you say his name is Mab? He doesn't sound like he's from round here.

Butty

He's not he's from Fleetwood. He moved here years ago hoping it would stop the visitations.

Dave

So his name is Mab and he's from Fleetwood?

Butty

Don't call him Fleetwood Mab. He hates Fleetwood Mac.

Mab, infuriated that nobody has done what he asked, marches forward yelling in gibberish whilst pointing the knife at them.

Mab

Karibstarum nich bik tach lalar! Karibstarum nich bik tach lalar! Karibstarum nich bik tach lalar! No talking and do as I ask. I'm fluent in Grey, Flatwood and Reptiloid. Now hands up, let me see your palms.

They do as instructed.

Mab

No webbed fingers; that's a good sign. Now drop your
trousers and turn around.

Dave

Not without buying me dinner first you don't.

Mab begins to pace back and forth, talking jibberish to
himself.

Mab

Karibstarum nich bik tach lalar! Karibstarum nich bik tach
lalar! Karibstarum nich bik tach lalar! Karibstarum nich
bik tach lalar!

John

What's he saying?

Dave

I think that's the German version of,
'Tell me lies tell me sweet little lies...'

John gives Dave a dig to shut him up.

Butty

It's Alien dialect John. Reptiloid if I'm not mistaken. Leave this to me.

Kachbit tan leetic dah Mab. Notek wag tailey. Notek wag tailey. Humanich.

Mab stops pacing, amazed that this man can speak Reptiloid.

Mab

You can speak Reptiloid? That must mean...

Butty

From Top Locks to the Water Tower we watch the skies....

Mab

Atop Churchill Mansions we stand with radios in hand...

Butty / Mab

Ready to act. Ready to protect. We are Alien's of Runcorn Spotters Elite. We are ARSE.

Mab

Butty?

Butty removes his helmet.

Butty

Hello Mab. Nice to see you.

Mab throws his arms around Butty and gives him an enormous hug.

EXT. APPROACHING CHURCHILL HALL – DAY

Butty and Mab approach the entrance of Churchill Hall; a small community centre situated to the side of a high rise tower block (Churchill Mansions) in Runcorn Old Town.

The streets are quiet with only a scattering of dead bodies. As Butty and Mab walk to the entrance of Churchill Hall, John and Dave slow down.

John

Do you think this is a good idea?

Dave

Got to trust your broski's instincts kid. This Fleetwood Mab fella. He's obviously a few grapes short of a fruit salad but I think we'll be alright. Just as long as he doesn't try to get our kecks off again.

Dave looks up to Churchill Mansions.

Dave

Churchill Mansions. What a shit hole. Somewhere, some cunt in a suit said 'I know what will solve Runcorn's housing crisis. I giant fucking concrete dildo. We'll fill it with poor people and leave them to rot. My only surprise is they never built more of the fuckers. Tell you what though, ace. If I had a top floor flat, I'd open the doors and wait for every dead fuck in the building to come then I'd throw them over the balcony. Secure the entrance and exits then I'd be King Dave, ruler of the massive concrete dildo.

Butty, at the entrance to Churchill Hall, signals for John and Dave to hurry.

John

Speaking of Dildos. Come on King Dave.

INT. CHURCHILL HALL. KITCHEN – DAY

A large cafeteria style kitchen, with stainless steel work tops and sinks. In a corner, inside a tin foil covered cardboard 'den' is a sleeping bag with blankets and a pillow and an old 1980s bullworker.

Mab, followed by the others enters.

Mab

Well, this is me. Make yourself at home. It's not much but it's everything I need. There's running water, the gas ovens work, that's my bed over there.

Butty

You're living here? What about your house?

Mab

Compromised. I was home when news broke about the zombie outbreak. They told us not to panic. To stay at home till it passed. But I knew what was really going on.

Butty

The meteor?

Mab

Exactly!

John

Hang on, what meteor? You've never mentioned a meteor?

Butty

You've never asked.

Mab

One week before the outbreak a meteor came crashing
down from outer space and landed in a lake in Russia.

Butty

The lake was the most polluted place on the planet. You
see years ago the Russian government filled the lake with
nuclear waste then covered it with concrete to stop
anything toxic escaping. It worked. For while.

Mab

Then 2 weeks ago the meteor hit, breaking through the
concrete.

Butty

A.R.S.E had been tracking it.

Dave

What in the name of Gary Numan, is A.R.S.E?

Mab

Aliens of Runcorn Spotters Elite? We're a crack team of alien and UFO experts. Sworn to protect the town and beyond from alien activity.

Dave

Yeah but, A.R.S.E?

John

You could have picked a name with a cool acronym? Something like, Runcorn Alien Protectors Elite?

Mab

R.A.P.E?

John

Yeah alright stick with A.R.S.E.

Butty

Following the meteor hitting there were reports of violent attacks. Starting in Russia then spreading across Europe at a rapid rate.

John

I don't remember seeing any of this on the news?

Mab

Well of course not. The mainstream media never reported a thing. The governments of this world wouldn't allow it.

Butty

They thought they could control it. Stop the outbreak before it was too late. They had no idea what they were dealing with.

Mab

Aliens!

John

That's not possible.

Mab

People didn't think the dead could walk the earth yet here we are.

Butty

A.R.S.E's theory is that the meteor carried alien bacteria.

Mab

Which, when mixed with the toxic waste in the Lake created a virus that caused the zombie outbreak.

Dave

Imagine the odds on a meteor carrying alien bacteria crash landing into toxic waste and causing a zombie outbreak? Must be a billion to one. Wish I'd put a nicker on that lar. I'd be quids in now.

Mab

Have you heard from other A.R.S.E. members? There's been no chatter over the airwaves for days now.

Mab moves away, opening cupboards and looking inside.

Butty

Not since the initial outbreak. We've had our hands full looking for my niece. The last person I spoke with was Skywatcher. You?

Mab

No, nothing.

Mab looks inside the cupboard. On the shelves are multiple tins of Spam and in between the tins, are a severed hand, some eyeballs and a human head; the same head that 80s Dave kicked off the shoulders of the zombie in episode 2. The others cannot see what Mab is looking at.

Mab turns to face the others with several tins of Spam in his hands.

Mab (CONT'D)

Dinner anyone?

INT. CHURCHILL HALL. HALL - DAY

John, Dave, Butty and Mab are sat around a table in the middle of the large hall. The table has a centre piece of a glass vase filled with dirty water and dead flowers. On plates are Spam served in various different ways.

Dave

Thanks for the food, ace.

Mab

Still plenty left. Spam and pineapple hedgehog anyone?

Dave

No thanks lar. Any more pork and you'll be popping an apple in my mouth and eyeing me for a hog roast.

Dave places a cigarette is mouth.

Mab

Erm, what do you think you're doing?

Dave

Smoking a tab. I always smoke after I've eaten.

John

Dave, you smoke after everything. A meal, a drink, a fart. You don't need a reason.

Mab

There's no smoking here. Look.

Mab points to a 'NO SMOKING' sign on the wall.

Mab

You'll have to go out.

Dave

Have a word with yourself soft lad. Dead fucks are roaming the streets and you want me to go outside for a smoke?

Mab

Rules are rules I'm afraid.

Dave

Yeah and zombies are zombies.

Mab

Smoking is bad for your health.

Dave

Zombies are bad for my health!

Mab

Maybe you should quit.

Dave

Can I smash his face in?

John

What about if he goes in the kitchen and cracks a window open? The smoke will go outside and Dave gets to enjoy a cigarette without the risk of being eaten alive.

Mab looks to Butty who nods back to suggest this is the best option.

Mab

Because you're a friend of Lone Wolf, I'll make an exception this time.

Dave

Cheers Fleetwood. I'll be back in a jiffy.

Mab

Don't touch anything!

Dave leaves

John

Lone Wolf? Who the hell do you think you are? Chuck Norris?

Butty

Alright, smart arse. It's a handle. Everyone that uses C.B. Radios has a handle.

Mab

It's how A.R.S.E communicate. We've been chatting over the airwaves for years.

John

So what's your handle?

Mab

Probe Magnet. Due to how many times I've been abducted. It's on my shirt, look.

Butty

It's a good set up you've got here my friend. Secure, spacious and in a good location for scavenging.

Mab

After I had to leave home this was the first place I thought of. This and the tower block next door, they are both mostly built from concrete. Which makes it perfect for blocking their scanning devises. I should have thought about living here years ago. It might have stopped all the abductions. Spam fries?

INT. KITCHEN

Dave is in the kitchen looking at how to open a window. He tries but it won't budge. He goes to light a cigarette anyway but before he does he hears a 'thud' coming from inside a broom cupboard.

INT. HALL

John

So, Lone Wolf and Probe Magnet... Jesus, you sound like a bad 70s cop show. You both believe that Aliens caused the zombie apocalypse?

Butty

I believe it's possible an alien organism, probably a
bacteria, was on the meteor and when it crashed and
mixed with the toxic waste in the lake, it mutated and
brought about the end of the world. But I think Mab has a
slightly different theory.

INT. KITCHEN

Dave goes to light his cigarette and hears the noise again.
He walks over to the broom cupboard and puts his ear to
the door.

Another thud.

INT. HALL

Mab

Oh it's not a theory Butty. I know what they're up to. This
was no accident. This plague was unleashed upon this
world to wipe us out. And when all of humanity has fallen
and all that's left are the living dead, they will arrive. To
claim this world as their own. It's the only plausible
explanation for all of this. Would anyone care for a spam
kebab?

Mab offers food to John and Butty whilst a commotion is heard in the kitchen.

Dave – Yelling from the kitchem

Ah fuck! Get back ya twat!

Butty and John rush from the table.

INT. KITCHEN

John, Butty and Mab enter to see a zombie shuffling out of the broom cupboard, attacking Dave. Dave has a frying pan as a weapon. The Zombie is Galactican, a member of A.R.S.E.

Mab

I told you not to touch anything!

Butty

Galactican?

John

What the hell is a Galactican?

Butty

He's a member of A.R.S.E.

Butty grabs a screwdriver from his tool belt.

Mab

No, don't kill Galactican. I need him!

Mab jumps between Butty and the zombie, which bites down on Mab's arm. He pushes the zombie away and recoils in pain whilst Dave moves in and pelts the zombie across the face with the frying pan. The zombie falls to the floor and Dave leans over, repeatedly bashing its head in until it is dead.

Dave lifts up the frying pan. Blood and brains are stuck to it.

Mab (CONT'D)

That's supposed to be none stick.

Butty and John help Mab over to his bed. They look at the bite mark on his arm.

Mab

Come on give to me straight. How bad is it? I can take it.

Dave

Well, on a scale of 1 to 10, I'd say you're fucked.

Mab

I don't want to die!

John

Dave, go and see if there is a medical kit anywhere?

Dave looks through the kitchen units.

Butty

What were you doing keeping a zombie like that?

Mab

He was my friend. A fellow A.R.S.E. I didn't want to put him down so I kept him. Then I realised that Galactican could be a link to the aliens. So I've been studying him to maybe find a way to end all this. And now he's gone.

Butty

And what did you find out?

Mab

Apart from the groans a lot and is a bit peckish for human flesh, not a lot.

Dave opens the cupboard with the body parts in.

Dave

Shit in my gob.

John

What is it?

Dave

Hey lads, you'll want to see this.

Butty and John join Dave and look inside the cupboard. John almost brings his Spam up.

Mab

It's not what it looks like.

John

That head looks familiar

Mab

I found it. Fell from the sky it did and landed right in front of me. It was the Reptiliods I'm telling you. The must have fired it at me from their spaceship. So I took it, to see if I can learn something from it. The hand was already there.

Oh Christ! It burns Butty. I can feel it inside me, running up my arm. Don't let me turn into one of them. It'll mean they've finally got me. Those damned Reptilians! They've been taking me for years and now they'll finally have me under their control!

John Pulls Butty and Dave away.

John

What shall we do about Mab? How long do you think he's got?

Butty

Hard to say. Could be minutes. Could be hours. But one thing is for sure, it will have to be me that does it. He's my Friend. I owe him a quick death. It's Just a question of how.

They return to Mab.

Mab

This is it then? My time's up? Which one of you is going to do it.

Butty

That would be me old friend. But how you die is up to you.

Mab

Oh thanks!

Dave

As Fleetwood Mac once said 'You can go your own way!"

John gives Dave a dig to shut him up.

Mab

There's only one way I'd like to go. And that is beaten to death with my old bullworker. I've had that since I was a boy and it was the only thing I took with me from my house. It's how I've kept it such good physical condition.

Butty Picks up the bullworker.

Mab

Will you make it quick, Butty? I don't want...

Butty bashes the bullworker into Mab's head repeatedly.

Dave

Is it OK if I smoke now?

EXT. CHURCHILL HALL – DAY

Butty followed by John and Dave, leave Churchill
Mansions.

Butty, alert and on patrol, walks ahead.

John

Well that was depressing!

Dave

Look on the bright side ace.

John

What bright side? Mab is dead!

Dave

Yeah, but I found a packet of ciggies on that Galactican fella so every cloud.

Dave lifts up the severed head.

Dave

Plus I've been reunited with me old mucka. Fancy a smoke lar? No? Thought so. Quitter!

Dave throws the head away.

John

What Butty and Mab were saying earlier about aliens causing the apocalypse? Do you think it's true?

Dave

These days lar, I'd say anything is possible. Maybe we should keep one eye on the sky from now on, kid. Come on.

John and Dave walk away from Churchill hall. A UFO hovers above the building before shooting up into the sky.

FADE IN:

EXT. CANAL – DAY

Butty, John and Dave are stood on the bank, looking at a canal boat.

Dave

Get in lar! Ever since Duran Duran made sailing cool in 1982, I've always wanted a boat!

Butty

Check the name John. If that isn't a sign I don't know what is.

John takes a closer look at the boat and sees that it is called Miss Emily.

Dave

This is fucking ace! I feel like Michael Douglas at the end of Romancing the Stone. All I need is some crocodile skin boots. Doubt I'll find any crocs in this canal though. Hey, can you skin a pike?

From inside the boat, a male zombie slams against the glass, gnawing at the window.

Dave (CONT'D)

There's always something isn't there? Hey lads, there's a
Dead Fuck on me boat!

Butty

I've got an idea.

Butty jumps on the boat and climbs on top of the cabin
above the door. The zombie is directly below him, inside
the cabin.

Butty (CONT'D)

Dave, open the door and I'll twat it.

Dave

Double team. I like it kid. You ready Butty lad?

Butty

Is the Pope Jewish?

Dave

No.

Butty

Just open the fucking door.

Dave opens the door and a zombie shuffles out. From atop of the cabin, Butty stabs a knife into the top of the zombie's head.

Dave

Nice! Come aboard John and help me throw this dead fuck overboard. Then I can straddle the nose of this boat and get my Simon Le Bon on.

Butty

It's called the bow, not the nose.

Dave

Whatever Captain Jack Spammo.

EXT. CANAL - DAY

We get a wide shot of the canal. Miss Emily sales passed. Butty is stirring the boat, john is inside the cabin looking out of the window with his head in his hands and Dave is straddling the bow, singing Rio by Duran Duran.

EXT. CANAL - DAY

The canal boat has been moored and Butty, John and Dave are walking away from it. Dave keeps looking back at the boat.

                    Dave

Are you sure she'll be OK? What if someone tries to have off with her? Have you tied her up properly? What if she drifts away? I'm not swimming in that canal to get it back. It's full of turds and shopping trollies. What if a horde of really fat zombies shuffle on board and the weight makes her sink? What if....

                    John

Dave! It's a fucking canal boat. A CANAL BOAT! Stop going on like it's a puppy you're leaving at home for the first time.

                    Dave

It's not just any canal boat. It's my canal boat. You haven't got a boat you wouldn't understand.

                    John

Dave, it's not your boat. We pinched it. It probably belonged to the poor bastard we found on board.

Dave

Yeah, but he was a dead fuck so I bagsied it.

John

Can we stop calling zombies dead fucks? They were once people after all, can we call them something a little bit more respectful?

Dave

Dead cunts?

Butty puts his hands out, stopping John and Dave from walking.

A female zombie approaches. She is wearing a power suit and dragging a travel suitcase behind her.

Dave

Look at the state of this. Dressed up like some high powered business women. I hate yuppies. Always chasing the fucking coin and what's the deal with the suitcase? They all drag those silly little suitcases with the massive handles around don't they? Suppose it makes them look important like they always have somewhere they need to be. A tenner says there's nothing inside but a make-up bag and a copy of Take a Break.

Behind her another high powered business zombie appears. Then another and another and another. A Mixture of male and female. They are all dragging travel suitcases.

John

Fucking hell it's The Apprentice!

Dave

I'm going to enjoy this.

Dave walks forward, swinging the Battle Paddle into the first female zombie's head. He picks up her travel suitcase and walks towards the next zombie, ramming it into its head, knocking it to the ground. Dave then continues to pound the zombies head into a bloodied pulp.

One of the other zombies is closing in on Dave.

Butty takes a catapult from his utility belt and fires a marble at the zombie, striking it in the forehead. We see the zombie hit the floor with a marble sized hole in its forehead.

Behind John another suit wearing zombie shuffles out of the bushes.

Dave (CONT'D)

Yuppy zombie at 12 O'clock!

John

What?

Dave

Bushes, knob head.

John turns to face the zombie. The zombie reaches out to grab John but he has lifted the hockey stick up to protect himself. Both John and the zombie have hold of the hockey stick; the zombie gnashing its teeth at John's face.

John pushes the hockey stick into the zombie, making it fall to the floor. Standing over the zombie John repeatedly bashes the zombie until it is dead.

John

Thanks for the help!

Butty

You had it little brother. Maybe there's hope for you yet.

Dave helps John up from the floor whilst something in the road ahead has caught Butty's attention. Both Dave and John notice what Butty is looking at. A large horde of zombies further up the road slowly approaches.

John

Right well that settles it then. Let's go this way.

Butty

There is no other way. Turn back and we'll add hours to our journey and it'll be dark soon. We don't want to be stuck outside after dark.

Dave

Better in the dark than dead lar. Unless you've got an awesomo plan to get through that horde of dead fucks... Sorry John, I mean... dead cunts, without being eaten alive.

Butty

I do actually. Here you go...

Butty reaches into a pocket on his utility belt and removes three perfume bottles.

Butty

Douse yourself in these.

Butty hands Dave and john a bottle of aftershave each; leaving one for himself.

John - Reading

Depression for Men, by Kalvin krevis.

Dave - Reading

Brown Rain by Paco Ra-bum.

John

What the hell are these, Butty?

Butty

I got those from Poundland. They are similar to your well-known brands but they stink to high heaven. So powerful that they can completely mask human scent. For a short while anyway. Should be enough for us to walk through without any trouble. This one's mine. It's from John Paul's goatee and it's called, Discharge.

John

You want us to spray this on ourselves and walk through that?

Butty

Yeah!

John

Are you fucking insane?

Dave

I think the verdict has been in for a while on that one, ace. How do you know this will work?

Butty

Trust me. It'll work.

John watches Butty and then Dave spray themselves with aftershave. John does the same and almost gags on the smell.

Butty (CONT'D)

Walk slowly and quietly. This will mask your smell but any noise might set them off. Dave, turn your Walkman off.

Dave

Oh what?

Butty and John give him a stern look and Dave reluctantly turns off his Walkman.

Butty

Follow my lead.

Butty followed by Dave and then John, walk towards the approaching horde, slowly and carefully in-between zombies, weaving their way through, occasionally spraying more aftershave on themselves.

After several tense minutes they make it through, walking passed the remaining zombies at the back of the horde.

John
I can't believe that worked.

Butty

Me neither.

John looks at him in disbelief

Dave

Sorry about this guys. I've been holding it in but I can't any longer.

Dave lets out a massive fart.

Dave (CONT'D)

Oh that's better.

Every zombie in the horde turns to look at the guys.

John

Leg it!

The three of them run away whilst the horde shuffles after them.

FADE IN:

EXT. ROAD - DAY

John, Dave and Butty run into view. Stopping to catch their breath.

Butty

I think we lost them.

John

I can't believe that worked.

Dave

I can't believe you made me turn my Walkman off! It never goes off. Ever. Not even when I'm sleeping.

Butty

It was a life or death situation Dave.

Dave

I know and that is the only reason why you're not eating battle paddle right now.

Butty

Look, we're here.

We see the Shopping City. A big shopping mall that looks like it's made from huge white building blocks.

Dave

The shopping city. I mean, does it look like a city to you? It looks more a block of Lego.

John

The land of Pound shops and frozen Food.

Butty

Hey, don't knock it little brother. The shopping city is the heart of the Runcorn community. It has been for a long time. Plus our Emily knows this place well.

John

She's worked a Saturday Job at Wilkos for a while now. You think she would come here?

Butty

Oh definitely, but not for Wilkos. No. She'll be heading to Poundland.

Dave

Poundland? What for? Bags of Werthers Originals and bottles of your Oder le Dead fuck?

Butty

Poundland is the greatest shop on Earth. Especially now the world has ended. Think about it. The gardening isle has all the weapons you will ever need. Shovels, hammers, spades. All perfect for hand to hand Zombie combat. Health care isle has baby wipes for keeping clean. The food isle is full of tinned and packaged foods with long best before dates. Pot Noodles, Corned beef, beans and of course, the king of Apocalypse food, Spam. It has it all. Then for entertainment you can head over to the toy section for a game of cards or even walk to the book section for a read of Shane Ritchie's autobiography. Perfect.

Dave

Good old Poundland eh? The Harrods of the North.

Butty

Follow me, I know a way in.

INT. SHOPPING CITY

We get long swooping shots of an empty shopping city.

John, Butty and Dave appear at an entrance to a walkway; closed shops on every side.

Dave

This is some creepy shit. We could be in Dawn of the Dead.

At the end of the corridor a female zombie appears. The zombie is wearing a onesie, has rollers in her hair and very badly drawn on eyebrows.

John

No, we are definitely in Runcorn!

Dave

This one's mine lads. I'm going to knock those eyebrows off her forehead.

Dave walks towards the zombie. The zombie shuffles towards Dave. It seems to take forever for them to reach each other.

Dave drills the paddle into the zombie's head. It falls to the floor and he bashes it several times for good measure. We see a shot of the zombie's battered head and the eyebrows are still intact.

John and Butty follow.

INT. SHOPPING CITY

The guys walk through the shopping City.

John

You know, I've never understood why Runcorn people
badmouth the shopping city. I love this Place.

Dave

I know, me too. It's that perfect blend of shite and
brilliant. A bit like Runcorn itself.

John

It's great. Just look around. Everything you could want
under one roof. You need the Post office? Go to the
Shopping City. You want a haircut? Shopping city. Food?
Shopping City.

Dave

Laugh at the locals? Shopping City. Sell your TV to Cash
Converters for drug money? Shopping City. Hey, there's a
Greggs up here. I might finally get a sausage Roll. Back of
the fucking net!

Butty

It's strange it's so quite. I was expecting more activity, specifically zombies. And look, every shop is closed up. The outbreak must have happened before anyone had chance to open the building. Apart from Scouse brows back there it looks empty. I think we should find a place to use as a base. Then we can split up and Search. See if we can find any signs that Emily has been here.

Dave

Can I go looting? I've always wanted to go looting.

Butty

I wouldn't. The shops are closed and probably alarmed. We set the alarms off and the noise will no doubt alert any Zombies close by.

Dave

Killjoy.

Butty

Come on, I know a place we can set up base.

INT. SHOPPING CITY

John, Dave and Butty are sat on a bench.

John

Is this the base then? I bench next to the toilets?

Butty

It's as good a place as any.

John

I miss my home. I miss coffee. I miss being clean. I've not had a wash for days. I've got sweat, dirt, blood and god knows what else on me. I'd give anything for a shower right now. Oh and my bed. I really miss my bed.

Butty

I don't miss anything. I quite like the world the way it is now. No more distractions you see. The only thing that matters now is survival.

John

Oh come on there must be something?

Butty

Well... I've learnt a lot from movies I suppose. A lot of my survival skills came from watching classics like Commando, Delta Force and Rambo. I guess I wouldn't be the man I am now if it wasn't for movies.

Dave

Movies. Pfft. I mean, fair enough if you're talking about the classics but Hollywood hasn't had an original idea for years, ace. It's all about greed these days. Selling nostalgia to bored middle aged fucknuggets that buy into anything that reminds them of a time when they didn't wish they were fucking dead. Makes me sick to my dick it does and do you know what? I'm glad the world ended because it means I'll no longer be bombarded by a shit stream of remake, re-hashes and re-imaginings. I'll tell you what though. If we ever get on top of this zombie apocalypse and things start to get back to normal, I'm going straight to Hollywood lar, and I'll show them how it's done. You know, I've never told anyone this but I've got idea for a movie so original it'll make Jerry Bruckhiemer and the rest of those big producer cocknockers shit their fucking pants. Do you wanna her it?

John

Not really.

Dave

So there's this bloke right. He's a loner. A drifter with a military background. He trained in combat and fucking deadly with his hands lar. Kung Fu and all that shit. And he's cool as fuck with awesome hair. One day he finds one of those fancy Virtual Reality headsets that are all the rage. But when he puts them on, the world and the people around him look different. He can see people for what they really are. Fucking aliens, kid. Masquerading as human's to infiltrate and take over the planet.

They're Here Trailer

The only man that can see them is the cool fuck drifter with phenomenal hair and VR glasses. Did I also mention how handsome he is and his dress sense is impeccable? Anyway, he soon figures out that these alien dipshits are up to no good and need taking care of so he gets some guns and takes care of business in true action hero style."

Dave stands and points his battle paddle forward like he's holding a machine gun.

Dave
I've come here to kick arse and smoke tabs. And I'm all out of tabs!

John

Hang on a minute, I think that's already a movie.

Dave

No it isn't.

Butty

It is. It's, They Live.

Dave

Fuck off, it's nothing like They Live.

Butty

It's exactly the same apart from your using a VR headset instead of sunglasses to see the aliens. You've ripped off John Carpenter.

Dave

(Realising his error)

Oh for fuck sake I have as well. What a bastard! I've been working on that idea for years too. Well that's totally fucking depressing. I'm going looting to cheer myself up. Anyone want anything?

Butty

No and listen, only loot shops that are open. Remember we don't want to set off any alarm. I'm going to go double check the entrances and exits and I'll try get some supplies whilst I'm at it. If I left it to you, you'd come back with a year's supply of cigarettes and a greatest hits of the 80s CD.

Dave

That hurt Butty? Why would you think I would stoop so low? I mean, steel a fucking shitty CD? I can't believe you'd think I would do such a thing. Cassettes all the way kid.

(Walking off)

A fucking CD...

Butty

Why don't you try and get some rest?

John

Do you think we're going to find her, Butty?

Butty

Oh without question. She's a lot more clued up than you think. You were so busy trying to be a good father, working every hour down at that mayonnaise factory, that you never stopped to realise how capable Emily is. She's not a little girl anymore John. She's tough and she's strong. All those weekends spent with her favourite Uncle have not gone to waste. Emily is as prepared for the end of the world as I am. I've made sure of it. She'll be out there now, surviving and kicking zombie arse. She's probably looking for us and we'll find each other soon enough. Now why don't you get some sleep and make the most of the quiet whilst Dave is off doing his shopping?

John

I will. I'll just nip to the toilet first. What about you?

Butty

I've not long been (tapping his drinks canister). Full to the brim. Oh you mean sleep. Hang one.

He crosses his eyes, holds his breath and has five seconds sleep.

Butty (CONT'D)

That should keep me going for a while. See you later.

Butty leaves. John shakes his head and walks off in the other direction.

We see 80s Dave strutting passed some shops, browsing the window displays.

Then we see Butty being stealthy, hiding behind walls, dashing about ready for action.

INT. TOILETS

John is sat on the toilet singing a song.

John

Toilet paper,

Toilet paper,

On a roll,

Next to me,

I could sue a few squares,

Maybe one or two squares,

How about three,

Hurray for me!

A harrowing groan echoes through the toilets.

JOHN (CONT'D)

Dave?

The groan is heard again.

JOHN (CONT'D)

Butty? Is that you?

The groan comes again. John pulls his pants up and grabs the door handle of the toilet cubicle.

JOHN (CONT'D)

Very funny guys. You nearly had me then.

John opens the cubicle door and pokes his head out, looking in both directions. There is nobody there. He shrugs it off, flushes the toilet and walks over to the sink and starts to wash his hands. He looks at himself in the mirror then leans over the sink, splashing his face with water. He lifts his head up and looks in the mirror again. Behind him is a zombie. John turns to face him. We see the zombie has his pants around his ankles and hanging below his shirt we can see his rancid ball bag and a long fetted penis. John panics, slips on water he has spilt and falls to the floor.

The zombie moves in, slipping on water also and falling on top of John. John's head is positioned between the zombie's legs and the rancid ball sack is touching his cheek with the fetted penis flopping about on his forehead. John screams.

John

Balls on my face. Balls on my face. I've got balls... on... my... FACE!

John tries to blow the cock and balls away but to no avail. The zombie slips and John ends up with a ball in his mouth and the nob resting over his eye. He begins to cry. Then we hear a squelch and the zombie stops groaning. Suddenly the zombie is thrown from John. We see 80s Dave looking down at John grinning like a lunatic.

Dave

There are a million and one things I could say right now and every single one of them would be fucking funny but nothing and I mean nothings tops seeing you being tea bagged by a zombie.

Butty walks into the toilets.

Butty

What was all that commotion?

Dave

It was your bro letting a zombie go balls deep in his mouth lar. What a moment to be alive.

John

I think I've got a pube in my mouth.

From outside, they hear zombie groans and a girl scream. The guys run out of the toilet to investigate.

INT. SHOPPING CITY

Butty, Dave and then John turn a corner and look down a long walkway of the shopping mall. Butty smiles and John looks shocked.

Butty

See little brother, I told you she'd be fine.

We see a girl, a hoody covering her face, brandishing 2 blood stained Poundland gardening forks. On the floor surrounding her lay 3 dead zombies. She pulls back the hoody and looks at the guys.

Emily

Hello dad.

END.

Printed by Amazon Italia Logistica S.r.l.
Torrazza Piemonte (TO), Italy

16429918R00105